Dragon's Rock

That day it came for him again.

Benjamin remembered leaning back
the motion of the train. And closing

The next moment it was upon him
through the landscape of his sleep. He
stifling heat of its breath, but it was no good. He could feel it
drawing closer, roaring its fury after him. Any moment now he
would have to face it and suffer for the wrong he sensed he had
done it.

He closed his eyes once more, but this time resisted sleep.
Sleep had become a place of fear, a place where the dragon
hunted him. But now he had a chance to go back, back to
Dragon's Rock and put things right. And perhaps then the
dragon would leave him alone.

Tim Bowler was born and brought up in Leigh-on-Sea, Essex,
the setting of his first novel, *Midget*, and he still visits there
regularly. Since leaving university, where he obtained an honours
degree in Swedish and Scandinavian Studies, he has worked in a
variety of fields including forestry and the timber trade and as a
teacher of modern languages. He now works as a freelance writer
and translator of Scandinavian languages and lives in Devon.
Dragon's Rock was his second novel for Oxford University Press.
He won the Carnegie Medal for his third novel, *River Boy*.

Dragon's Rock

Other books by Tim Bowler

Midget
River Boy
Shadows
Storm Catchers

Dragon's Rock

Tim Bowler

Oxford University Press

Oxford New York Toronto

OXFORD
UNIVERSITY PRESS

Great Clarendon Street, Oxford OX2 6DP

Oxford University Press is a department of the University of Oxford.
It furthers the University's objective of excellence in research, scholarship,
and education by publishing worldwide in

Oxford New York

Auckland Bangkok Buenos Aires
Cape Town Chennai Dar es Salaam Delhi Hong Kong Istanbul
Karachi Kolkata Kuala Lumpur Madrid Melbourne Mexico City Mumbai
Nairobi São Paulo Shanghai Taipei Tokyo Toronto

Oxford is a registered trade mark of Oxford University Press
in the UK and in certain other countries

First published 1995
First published in this paperback edition 2002

British Library Cataloguing in Publication Data available

ISBN 0 19 275219 7

3 5 7 9 10 8 6 4 2

Printed in Great Britain by
Cox & Wyman Ltd, Reading, Berkshire

For my Mother and Father

'That only which we have within, can we see without.
If we meet no gods, it is because we harbour none.'

RALPH WALDO EMERSON

1

That day it came for him again.

He remembered leaning back and resting, and rocking to the motion of the train. And closing his eyes.

The next moment it was upon him, racing like an angry fire through the landscape of his sleep. He ran, gasping for air in the stifling heat of its breath, but it was no good. He was already starting to weaken, starting to give up. And he could feel it drawing closer, closer, roaring its fury after him. Any moment now it would appear, any moment now he would have to face it and suffer for the wrong he sensed he had done it. Any moment now he would—

'The next station will be Exeter St Davids. Exeter St Davids the next station. Thank you.'

He blinked his eyes open, unsure for a moment whether he was still dreaming.

But there was no dragon before him. Only a man watching him over the top of his newspaper.

'Are you all right, lad?'

'What . . . what do—?'

'You were moaning while you were asleep.'

He looked out of the window at the fields rushing past.

'I'm all right, it's just . . . just—'

'A bad dream maybe.'

'Yes,' he said quickly. 'A bad dream. And something . . . '

He stared over the wintry land as far as the horizon.

Something I've got to put right.

He closed his eyes once more, but this time resisted sleep. Sleep had become a place of fear, a place where the dragon hunted him; and so it had been since that first fateful visit

1

six years ago. But now he had a chance, to go back and put things right, and start to live again. And perhaps then the dragon would let him be.

He opened his eyes again, ignored the man's quizzical glance and looked up at the sky, and for a while found his mind drifting away from the dragon. To the farm, the fields, the forest, his nervousness about seeing Toby again; but most of all to the things that had haunted him since that visit. The things he had seen but would never forget.

And one in particular, though he'd glimpsed it for but a second.

The face of a frightened woman.

The knife flashed and Toby smiled as he often did when he was whittling and found he'd poked his tongue out. But then whittling needs concentration, he decided, and you can't concentrate without poking your tongue out.

Chip, chip, chip.

The bits flew down on the grass, and he smiled again. There was always something reassuring about the feel of wood. He glanced at the sheep-dog curled at his feet.

Feigning sleep probably but he knew Flash would only need a sniff of action to be up and bounding. For a moment he stopped whittling and watched the slow movement of the stomach, in and out, regular and relaxed, as though nothing were really wrong after all. As if to remind him of reality, he heard his father call.

'Toby!'

He looked over his shoulder towards the paddock fence.

'Here!'

'What are you doing?'

'Whittling.'

'Is Flash with you?'

He wished Dad wouldn't keep asking, even if it was for the best of reasons.

'Yes!'

2

He heard his father thrust something into the shed, then close the door and clip the latch. A moment later he appeared round the corner, his arms bare despite the December chill.

'Good, I thought he might have . . . you know—'

'He's been with me for the last hour.'

As though sensing they were talking about him, Flash rolled over on his back, looking from one to the other. Dad bent down and ran his hand through the fur.

'You think I'm being over-cautious, don't you? But you know what he's like for running off.' He nodded towards the western fields. 'Specially that way. We can't take any chances. I saw her on our land again this morning when I was out. She was watching him.'

'Gordon saw her yesterday.'

'So we've got to be careful. You ready?'

'Suppose so.'

'Come on, it won't be that bad and you promised you'd try. We'd better get going. We don't want to be late.'

Yes, we do, Toby thought, but he followed Dad through the gate and down the muddy path to the house.

'Do it for your mum and me,' Dad said, stopping by the door. 'I mean, you wouldn't like it if you were stuck at a boarding-school in England while we were away in Hong Kong. You wouldn't want to spend Christmas on your own.'

'But you said they'd have paid for him to go out to Hong Kong for Christmas.'

'They gave him the choice. Said if he wanted, they'd pay for him to fly out, otherwise he could stay with us since we'd offered to put him up.'

'So why isn't he going out there?'

'Because he particularly wanted to come here. He said so.'

'But why?'

'I don't know.' Dad looked at him tetchily. 'Look, we've been through all this.'

3

Mum's face appeared round the door.

'Where's Flash? Is he with you?'

As though in reply the dog bounded into the house and through to the kitchen. Dad watched for a moment, then reached inside the door for his coat.

'Right, Toby.'

Totnes Station had a deserted air. Toby looked up and down the platforms but apart from Dad and himself, there was no one to be seen. The little café was shut, the waiting-room was empty, there were no sounds of movement or voices; it might have been a ghost station, waiting for a spectral train that would never come.

He frowned.

This train would come.

He looked down the track and to his relief saw no sign of it. A pied wagtail flitted over the station fence and ran along the track for a few yards before flying off again. He pulled his coat collar up and burrowed his chin deeper.

'Half-past three,' said Dad. 'Train's late.'

Toby glanced up and saw the sky already darkening. Let it be late, he thought, let it never come, let it go somewhere else. Then he heard the tinkling in the rails.

He cocked his head to one side and listened, wondering whether Dad had heard it too. A door banged behind them and a station official strode past them to the edge of the platform.

' 'Nother cold day,' said Dad.

The man peered down the line for a few seconds, but eventually managed a nod.

'We'll have a white Christmas yet.'

There was the train; he could see it now, a huge, hateful serpent snaking its way towards them until finally the engine and the first of the carriages swept past the platform. He glared at it, wishing it would rattle on to Plymouth without stopping.

4

But it slowly came to a halt; and now all he could pray for was that no one would get off. But that was certainly too much to hope.

Dad started forward.

'There he is.'

A door had opened and a small figure was climbing down.

Toby stared, trying to remember the picture in his mind of six years ago. The hair was longer, but it was still the same revolting blond, and even from here he could see the pale, unhealthy-looking skin. And the glasses were even more ridiculous than the last ones he had.

Dad bustled ahead.

'Benjamin! Welcome! Toby, get that suitcase.'

Toby was still studying Benjamin and he found he liked what he saw even less than last time. He's still got that funny way of looking past you, he thought, not meeting your eyes properly, and—

'Toby! Suitcase!'

Benjamin's lip quivered.

'It's all right, I can—'

Toby reached up and took the suitcase.

'No problem.'

'Thank you,' said Benjamin.

They set off down the platform, Toby hanging back slightly and watching with amusement as Benjamin struggled to keep up with Dad's vigorous pace.

'How's boarding-school?' he heard Dad say.

'Not very nice. Did . . . did you have to wait long?'

'Couple of minutes.'

'Ten!' Toby called.

He ignored the backward glance from his father and continued to study Benjamin.

It was pathetic.

He was out of breath already, panting and gasping like on a cross-country run, and he wasn't even carrying his suitcase. The prospect of Christmas and two weeks of Benjamin looked bleaker than ever.

They had reached the exit now and, as Toby expected, there was an interminable wait while Benjamin looked for his ticket, first trying this pocket, then that, before eventually finding it stuffed inside his handkerchief. But at last they were out of the station and heading up the road.

Even that was too good to be true. They hadn't gone ten yards before Benjamin stopped.

'Haven't you got . . . ?'

Dad looked round.

'Something wrong?'

'I just thought . . . maybe you'd have a car with you.'

Toby rolled his eyes. Fifteen miles from home and he thinks we're travelling on foot; this is going to be even worse than last time. Dad nodded up the road.

'We've got a car. See?'

'Isn't that a Land Rover?'

Toby saw the first sign of frustration on Dad's face, but the voice resolutely betrayed none of it.

'That's right, a Land Rover. Seen better days too, but it'll get us home. Right, Toby?'

'Nothing posh in our family.'

'Of course not.' Benjamin nodded quickly, as though anxious to show agreement.

Dad walked over to the driver's door and started to unlock it. Benjamin turned to Toby.

'Your father—'

'What about him?'

'He . . . he looks different.'

'Lost some hair probably.'

Benjamin's eyes slanted away towards the sky.

'He was nice to me last time. He gave me a ride on the tractor.'

Toby looked at the face before him, the wispy curls of hair blowing girlishly round it, and wondered what he'd done to deserve seeing this every day for the next two weeks. It certainly hadn't improved with time, he decided;

it was still a baby-face, a weak face, a nothing face. A face he could do without.

He ran ahead, pulled open the side door of the Land Rover and climbed in, dragging the suitcase after him. Dad was already in the driver's seat.

'Toby, push that case to the side, can you? Benjamin can't get in. And squeeze up.'

'I can go in the back.'

'Not with all the fencing stuff, you can't.'

'I can! I can climb over the top.'

'Do as you're told.'

He moved reluctantly to the right and pulled the suitcase away from the opening. Dad leaned across him.

'Right, Benjamin, jump in.'

Some jump, Toby thought, watching Benjamin cautiously lift one leg in, slide his body after it until he was sitting almost hunched up on the seat, then with equal caution lift the other leg in and close the door. Dad started the engine, swung the Land Rover round and they headed off up the road.

The sky had darkened further and as they pulled out of Totnes, Toby leant back and gazed upwards at the dusky islands of cloud, listening uninterestedly to Dad's attempts at conversation; asking Benjamin about the journey, why he didn't like school, how his parents would manage Christmas without him.

They're lucky, Toby thought. They're probably glad they haven't got him. And we're stuck with him instead.

The fields were soon racing past and Totnes behind them. It was good to be heading home to a warm house, even if they did have an unwanted guest with them. Dad seemed finally to have run out of questions, and since Benjamin asked none of his own, the journey was becoming slightly more bearable. At last they were off the main road and cutting along the old familiar lane towards the farm.

Dad, looking more and more at ease the closer they drew to home, caught Benjamin's eye and nodded out of the

7

window. 'See that line of poplars, Benjamin?'

Benjamin stared blankly ahead and Toby chuckled. But Dad heard.

'No need for that, Toby. We weren't all born in the country.' He pointed over the field. 'See those trees, Benjamin?'

Benjamin nodded.

'They're called poplars. Now just beyond, you should see some buildings. Got them?'

'Yes, sir.'

''S all right, none of that "sir" rubbish. I don't get any airs and graces from Toby, so I don't expect any from you. Anyway, see the buildings?'

'Yes.'

'That's the farm next to ours.'

'The one with the geese?'

'You've got a good memory after six years. What else can you remember?'

Toby saw the lips quiver again in that annoying way.

'I remember lots of things,' said Benjamin. 'Lots of things. I . . . '

The pallid eyes assumed an inward look and Benjamin's voice trailed away as though it had never been.

Toby stared. This boy was weird; even weirder than last time. They drove on in silence and he found himself thinking about Flash again, wishing he'd locked the dog up before leaving. But perhaps Mum had him indoors, or Gordon was with him, or—

He leaned forward, impatient to get home and make sure all was well. Dad pointed again.

'Remember that, Benjamin?'

Benjamin squinted out of the window.

'The oak tree?'

'There you are, Toby, he does know a bit about trees.'

Benjamin took off his glasses and wiped them nervously.

'I only remember the oak tree because you told me about it last time I came.'

8

'Did I?'

'Yes. You were standing by it, and you were wearing a dark blue pullover—a big woolly one—with a funny pattern—'

'The things you remember.'

'—And you told me it's the old oak that guards the house whenever you're away.'

'Did I say that?'

'Yes. You had a hat on, too, a funny flat one.'

'I can't let you stay with us if you're going to be rude about what I wear.'

Benjamin flushed.

'I . . . I didn't mean to—'

Dad winked at him.

'I'm only pulling your leg. You can make as many jokes as you want about my appearance. Everyone else does.'

Benjamin carefully replaced his glasses and seemed on the point of answering; then, without a word, he turned suddenly and stared out over the field. Toby watched and frowned, wondering what could possibly have attracted Benjamin's attention out there. Probably nothing at all, he decided, or nothing of any interest. But he noticed that Benjamin had started almost imperceptibly to shake.

He ignored Benjamin and looked about him; there was something far more important to think about and he wouldn't be happy until he was home and everything was all right. They were through the farm entrance now and bumping along past the orchard towards the house; too early to feel anxiety, he knew, but he felt it just the same and wished Dad would drive faster. They entered the yard, pulled up outside the door and Dad switched off the engine.

And Toby's anxiety grew.

Inevitably Benjamin was taking his time getting out.

'Come on,' said Toby. 'We haven't got all day.'

'Give him a chance,' said Dad. 'And don't forget to take his case in.'

Benjamin climbed clumsily out. Dad laughed.

'Don't worry about Toby. He's always a man in a hurry. He's probably forgotten to make your bed or something.'

Toby was already out of the Land Rover and running towards the house.

'Toby!' Dad called after him. 'Suitcase!'

Toby whirled round and saw Benjamin smiling shyly at him.

'I can . . . get it.'

'No bother,' he said huffily, ran back and grabbed the case, and raced towards the house so fast that he almost barged into Mum coming out.

'Careful, Toby,' she said and quickly stepped past him. 'Now, where is he, where is he? Benjamin!'

Toby stopped to look, despite his impatience, and immediately wished he hadn't. Benjamin was gazing up at her, a simpering smile round his lips, and she was smiling back, her arm round his shoulder as though she actually liked him.

'It's lovely to see you again,' she said. 'We've been so looking forward to having you with us for Christmas. Six years has been too long.'

She drew him towards the house, her arm still round his shoulder.

'We'll have lots to talk about and lots of things for you to do.'

Toby recognized the tone of her voice: it was the one she used when she spoke to animals or little children; which seemed appropriate here, he thought grimly. Anyway, Benjamin was obviously enjoying it. But this wasn't the time to stand around.

He dashed into the house. From the oven came the tempting smell of baking bread and he saw three loaves already on the kitchen table, each one prickly with sunflower seeds. The clock in the hall chimed reassuringly. Everything seemed normal.

But everything was not normal. He knew that. He

10

dropped the suitcase, ran to the window and scanned the yard, listening intently. Behind him he heard Mum and Benjamin come in.

'You remember Gordon?' she was saying. 'Toby's brother?'

'Yes, he's got a big brown coat.'

She laughed.

'Well, he did have. Anyway, he's nineteen now. He works on the farm with us. He should be around somewhere.'

Gordon! Toby stroked his chin. Maybe that was it. Then he heard Dad call from outside.

'Has anyone seen . . . ?'

But his father's voice died away. And as it did so, Toby saw the bulky figure of his brother at the far end of the paddock, walking towards the house.

Carrying something in his arms.

2

Toby sat on the paddock fence, kicking his legs back and forth, glad the darkness had come. He hated crying; it made him feel he was weak and childish, like Benjamin.

Benjamin. Stupid Benjamin. He could imagine Benjamin crying; he almost wanted to see Benjamin crying. He heard footsteps behind him but didn't need to turn to see who it was.

'Come inside, Toby,' said Dad. 'You've got to eat.'

He ran his eyes over the silver birch, its trunk shiny in the moonlight. Dad touched his shoulder.

'Let's have a walk at least.'

He climbed off the fence and followed Dad away from the house, and they walked in silence for a few minutes. The evening air was growing colder. Dad stopped to light his pipe, eyeing Toby over the flame of the match.

'I know how you feel. It's tough losing a dog. It's like losing a friend.' He shook the match and blew out a cloud of smoke. 'Reminds me of old Socks.'

'Socks?'

'Didn't I tell you about Socks? He was my dog when I was a kid. Sheep-dog, same as Flash. Bit bigger maybe. I lost him when I was fourteen.'

'Why Socks?'

'Can't you guess? He had these funny white bits at the bottom of his legs, like a pair of socks.'

'Two pairs for a dog.'

'Right. Two pairs.'

'Did he die the same way as Flash?'

'In a trap? No, thank God, least I hope not. I don't really

know how he died. There were some gypsies camping near the farm and they took a fancy to him. When they moved on, he moved on too.'

'Did you see them take him?'

Dad thumbed his pipe.

'Not as such but I always reckoned he went with 'em. He was just like Flash, too sociable for his own good.'

Toby looked down.

'But we know who did this.'

'Maybe we do, but we can't prove anything.'

'We can. It could only be her. Gordon said it wasn't a normal trap, it was some horrible thing cobbled together, and if it hadn't been so huge, it probably wouldn't have killed Flash outright when he—' he shuddered, '—when he put his nose in to sniff it. And Gordon saw her standing over it. How much more proof do you need?'

Dad shook his head.

'Technically, the police could say she was just looking. And there's no hard evidence. The trap's gone, Gordon said. He's just been back to look for it.'

''Cause she took it, that's why. To cover up. You know it's her.'

Dad turned back towards the house.

'It still won't stand up as proof. Come on, let's join the others. We've got a guest to look after.'

Toby felt his fists tighten.

Supper should have been a joyous event: his favourite rolls, crusty brown and speckled, and a tantalizing smell of herbs and vegetables from the soup in the tureen. And Christmas to look forward to.

But there was no joy tonight. And for some reason, despite the fire, the room felt curiously chill.

The others took their normal places, Dad at the head, Mum at the foot, and Gordon opposite. To his annoyance, he saw a place laid to his left.

'We're putting you there, Benjamin,' said Mum. 'Next to Toby.'

'Thank you,' said Benjamin.

'So you can give Toby a kick,' said Gordon, 'when he slurps his soup.'

'Very funny,' said Toby.

He glanced at Benjamin and to his surprise saw he had his eyes closed. He looked at Mum.

'What's he doing? Praying or something?'

'Ssh!' Mum put a finger to her lips, and quietly reached for the tureen. At the sound of the lid moving, Benjamin's eyes opened.

'Oh.' He looked startled. 'We've . . . we've started.'

'No, we haven't,' said Mum. 'Pass me your bowl.'

Benjamin studied it for a moment before holding it out.

'You had these last time. I remember the pattern.'

'That's right.' She filled the bowl and handed it back. 'Not as many though. We've broken a few since then.'

'He's got a good memory,' said Dad. 'Remembers all kinds of things.'

Gordon held out his bowl.

'Shame he's not staying during school time. He could help Toby with his homework. When Toby does homework, that is. Thanks, Mum.'

Toby ignored the leg pull and turned to Benjamin.

'What were you doing just now?' he said bluntly.

Benjamin's lip trembled again.

'What—?'

'You had your eyes closed. What were you doing?'

Mum touched him on the arm.

'Let Benjamin get started on his soup.'

Toby heard Dad clear his throat and knew a reprimand was coming. But Benjamin spoke first.

'I didn't know I had my eyes closed.' He looked from face to face. 'I just—'

'You don't need to explain anything,' said Mum. She glanced at Toby. 'Let's just eat, shall we?'

14

'Good idea,' said Gordon.

Toby kept his eyes from the others, sensing their disapproval. They started eating and for some time nobody spoke, then, to his annoyance, he heard Benjamin's voice again.

'Who's that lady?'

He looked up angrily and caught Gordon's eye; but his brother casually dipped a piece of bread in his soup.

'What lady's that, Benjamin?'

'The lady I saw in the field as we were coming into the farm.'

Toby played with his spoon, making patterns in the soup.

'Sure you didn't have your eyes closed?' he said.

'Don't be rude, Toby,' said Dad. 'Eat your soup.'

You don't eat soup, he thought rebelliously, you drink it. But this wasn't the time to answer back. He reached for another roll and let the others talk on.

'She's got a very nice face,' said Benjamin. 'Who is she?'

Toby saw his parents exchange glances.

'Some lady out walking,' said Mum.

Dad nodded.

'Must have been. Obviously wasn't her.'

'Who?' said Benjamin. 'Obviously wasn't who?'

Again they exchanged glances; but it was Gordon who spoke.

'The Wild Woman.'

Benjamin sat up, his face twitching.

'Who's the Wild Woman?'

Dad cleared his throat again.

'Just a vagrant. Turns up from time to time. Bit unusual.' He took another roll and reached for the butter. 'Best to keep out of her way if you see her.'

Toby almost snorted. It was pointless Dad trying to sound casual when he was such a hopeless actor. He wondered whether Benjamin had sensed what he was not being told.

15

'What does she look like?' said Benjamin.

'You'll know her,' said Gordon. 'She's not called the Wild Woman for nothing.'

'Don't frighten him,' said Mum. 'Benjamin, you probably won't see her and if you do, one of us'll be with you. Let's leave it now.'

But Benjamin's face was alive with questions.

'Where does the Wild Woman live?'

'Nowhere special,' said Gordon. 'Like Dad says, she's a vagrant. But they do say she's got some kind of a . . . lair.'

Toby listened sullenly. Now it was Gordon trying to sound casual, and he was no more convincing than Dad.

Benjamin's eyes misted.

'What's it like? Her lair.'

'Don't even know there is a lair,' said Gordon. 'That's just what people say.'

'Is it a ruined house at the top of a valley? With a rock down below?'

Gordon stared at him.

'How do you know that?'

Benjamin's eyes misted further and the lids half-closed, as though to block out all distraction from his thoughts.

'I've been there,' he said softly. 'What's it called?'

Toby leaned close to Benjamin's ear, meaning to shout and startle him from his reverie; but he found he could only whisper.

'Dragon's Rock.'

After the meal Mum stood up.

'Right, who wants tea? Benjamin?'

Toby looked across and wondered whether Benjamin had heard; the opacity in the eyes was still there and he hadn't spoken for the rest of the meal. But he stirred suddenly and even smiled.

'Have you got any of that hot chocolate you had last time? In the red jar, on the shelf by the cooker.'

She laughed.

'Yes, want some?'

'Yes, please.'

'Toby?'

'Tea, please. In the black jar, on the shelf by the sink.'

He regretted his words at once; there was only one person he wanted to hurt, and it wasn't Mum.

'Sorry,' he said quickly.

'Make yourself useful and clear away these things.'

'I can help,' said Benjamin.

'Thank you. Later on we can go and decorate the Christmas tree. Tea for everybody else?'

'Yes, please,' said Gordon.

Dad was poking the fire and merely nodded. Toby watched him for a moment, wondering why no one had mentioned the strange chill in the room. He stacked the empty bowls on top of each other and followed Mum through to the kitchen, then, as she prepared the drinks, he walked back and forth, bringing the supper things through.

Each time he entered the dining-room the coldness seemed to have deepened.

Gordon and Dad were by the fireside, talking farm business. Benjamin had obviously forgotten his offer to help and was wandering about the room, gazing, it seemed, at nothing in particular.

Back in the kitchen he found Mum washing up.

'The dining-room's cold,' he said.

'Put some more logs on the fire, then. Dry the tureen first, can you, and make some space for the other things.'

He reached for it, glad to have something to do.

'Mum, why's Benjamin . . . I mean—?'

'Why's he the way he is?' She shook her head. 'Why are you the way you are?'

'But he's weird.'

She stopped washing up for a moment.

'You can't see the world through his eyes. You've got to be patient when people don't act the way you do.'

17

He rubbed hard at the tureen.

'I just don't like him. I don't like him at all. There's something creepy about him.'

'What you mean is, you don't understand him. But you must try. He's a guest in our house. He probably finds it just as difficult to understand you, or any of us. We lead a very different life to him.' She smiled. 'I think you can safely say that tureen is done.'

He put it down and reached for a plate.

'No,' she said. 'Take the tea through. It's brewed. I'll bring Benjamin's hot chocolate. I can finish the drying later.'

The fire was roaring now and the dining-room felt slightly warmer. Benjamin still wandered about, his eyes staring as before, though at what, Toby could only guess. Dad looked up from the fireside.

'Gordon wants to go out tomorrow and check over some of the fencing, in case there's any damage after the gale last week, and he thought it might be nice to give Benjamin a ride on the tractor at the same time. Show him some of the farm again.'

'Right.'

Gordon kicked off his slippers and stretched.

'Suppose you'll be tagging along. If you're not too busy whittling or something.'

Toby said nothing. It wasn't that he minded Gordon making fun of him, but no one seemed to be thinking about Flash any more. He watched Benjamin furtively; nothing had been right since he arrived, and now here he was, drifting about the room, acting funny.

As if to contradict him, Benjamin stopped by the window.

'I'd love to go out on the tractor tomorrow,' he said.

'Fine,' said Gordon. 'Let's hope it doesn't tip down on us.'

Benjamin's face clouded.

'Do tractors do that?'

Gordon laughed.

'I mean the rain. Let's hope the rain doesn't tip down on us. Or the snow for that matter. Looks like we might be in for a bit.'

Toby shivered and moved closer to the fire. Then Benjamin spoke again.

'Why do you light the fire when it's so hot in here?'

Toby looked round and saw Benjamin's cheeks flickering like flames.

'Hot?' he scoffed. 'How can you say you're hot?'

He heard Mum's voice behind him.

'You're probably tired, Benjamin. You've had a long journey and it wasn't the happiest of arrivals.'

'I am a bit,' he said.

'Well, why don't you turn in? Come on, I haven't shown you where everything is in your room. We can do the Christmas tree tomorrow.'

'I thought I was going to have some hot chocolate.'

She held up the mug she was holding and he smiled.

'Thank you.' He walked up to her and took it. 'That lady in the field—I saw her last time I came. I wish I knew why she's so frightened.'

And without another word, he walked past her and up the stairs.

Toby watched Mum follow, then turned and looked over the room. Dad had lit his pipe and Gordon was reading the newspaper, and both seemed contented enough and unperturbed by Benjamin's latest remark.

But the room still felt cold.

He walked through to the kitchen and opened the back door, and gazed out over the yard towards the paddock. The place where Flash loved to play.

There would be no stars tonight.

Benjamin woke in the early hours, sweating from the nightmare of the dragon, and for a few seconds of anguish

19

he lost all memory of where he was. He threw out an arm in panic and it brushed back the curtain a few inches; and he saw the slumberous fields stretching away into the darkness.

Recollection returned, and with it some relief. But for the first time the suspicion arose within him that the dragon had ceased to be a figment of his sleep; that it was now no fiction, no falsehood, no illusion, but had somehow broken the fetters of his mind and was even at this moment prowling through the night.

3

'Jump on!' shouted Gordon, looking down from the tractor.

Toby gave a curt nod to Benjamin, standing awkwardly in the mud, his new boots already dirty.

'You first.'

Benjamin stepped forward, hesitantly searching for handholds.

'Here.' Gordon reached down. 'Put your feet there, that's right, and pull yourself up on this.' Benjamin climbed slowly up. 'Toby? Come on!'

Toby jumped on as nonchalantly as he could manage, noting the look of admiration from Benjamin.

'Show-off,' said Gordon.

He started the engine and pulled out of the yard onto the track. Toby settled back, glad that the roar of the engine gave him an excuse not to talk.

Gordon was pointing things out to Benjamin, who was leaning close to hear. Toby watched for a few moments, wishing Benjamin wouldn't keep nodding his head as Gordon spoke, then an idea occurred to him and he touched Benjamin on the shoulder.

'How old are you?' he shouted.

Benjamin turned. 'Fourteen.' He paused, as though frightened to offend. 'How old are you?'

'Nearly fifteen.'

Gordon laughed. 'Nearly fifteen!'

'Well, I am!'

'You're fourteen, same as Benjamin. You're not fifteen till you're fifteen.'

'Shut up!'

But Gordon only laughed again.

The tractor was bouncing now that the ground was more uneven and Gordon leaned forward to concentrate on the driving.

Toby shivered, the chill of the breeze adding to the frosty crispness of the morning. Then he noticed Benjamin stroking something in his hand.

'What's that?'

Benjamin flushed.

'You mean . . . ' He held out his hand with some reluctance. 'You mean this?'

'A stone? Is that all it is? I thought it was something important, the way you were stroking it.'

Benjamin's mouth quivered again.

'I found it last time I came.'

'Let me see it.'

'Well, I—'

'Come on!'

'It's only a stone.'

'So let me see it!'

Toby checked to make sure Gordon was leaning too far forward to see or hear, then snatched the stone; and now that he'd seen Benjamin's reluctance to hand it over, he decided to hold on to it as long as possible.

'What do you keep stroking it for?'

'I just do.'

'So where did you find it?'

Benjamin's eyes were fixed on the stone.

'At Dragon's Rock,' he said.

Toby tried to ignore the apprehension he always felt at the mention of Dragon's Rock and to enjoy instead the anxiety in Benjamin's undeviating stare, not to mention the curious beauty of the stone itself. He was beginning to see why Benjamin liked it: it was a strange violet colour, long and slim and tapering at one end, and while the sides felt smooth and almost silky, the base was flat and sharp

22

against his finger. He pondered the contrast, as he let the stone play over his fingers.

So smooth and so sharp.

One side to soothe, and one side to cut.

He looked up and saw Benjamin's eyes still on the stone; and suddenly he found himself fighting the desire to drop it. Accidentally on purpose, of course.

But perhaps not yet.

He tossed it in the air a couple of times, noting with satisfaction the consternation on Benjamin's face, then he closed his fist round it and pretended to throw it away.

Consternation turned to panic. He grinned and, before Benjamin could call out and alert Gordon, opened his hand to reveal the stone still there.

'Give it back,' said Benjamin.

Toby glanced at Gordon again. But all was well: he was still leaning forward and hadn't heard anything. He tried to think of an excuse for keeping the stone longer.

'You still haven't told me why you stroke it.'

The tractor rode a bump in the field and Benjamin put a hand behind his back to steady himself.

'I just do.'

And before Toby had time to think, he grabbed the stone and thrust it in his pocket.

Toby watched suspiciously, almost wishing he'd never seen the stone. But as they jolted down the field, an idea started to form in his mind.

The tractor ride went on too long and Toby was soon bored and ready to jump off. Tractor rides were only a novelty for townies. He cast an eye over Gordon's huge shoulders, the thick black hair only partially covering the somewhat elephantine ears that everyone joked about, no one more so than Gordon himself. Unable to resist, he reached out and flicked one of them.

Gordon didn't bother to look round.

'Watch it, Toby!' he called. 'Or you'll be sitting on a cow-pat.'

'How d'you know it wasn't Benjamin?'

'Benjamin's got manners.'

'I've got manners.'

'First I've heard of it.'

They were close to the bottom fence now and he could see the rows of young larch that Dad had planted along to the right. The final stretch was the bumpiest of all but at last they were there. He jumped straight down and ran up the field, glad to be moving.

Gordon's voice rang out.

'Hoy! Toby! Grab some of the stuff, will you?'

He ran back and stood by the tractor, blowing his hands.

'Bring this.' Gordon handed him the old bucket-bag they used for carrying tools and tramped over to the fence with the wire under his arm. Toby followed and stood by while his brother bent over one of the posts.

A huge raven wheeled overhead only a few feet from them, and glided away over the larch trees. Toby watched until it disappeared from view.

'Not much wrong here,' said Gordon, straightening up.

'Dad was right then, about you fussing over nothing.'

'He only says that 'cause he's got other jobs he wants me to get on with. But I still reckon some bits of the fencing need looking at after the gale.'

'We going then?'

'No, I've got a bit of work to do here. You and Benjamin can buzz off for a while.' He looked round suddenly. 'Hang on, where's he got to?'

Toby scanned the field, then pointed.

A hundred yards away, Benjamin stood gazing over the fence towards the lower ground to the south.

'He's really peculiar,' he said.

'Doesn't mean any harm,' said Gordon. 'Give him a chance. We weren't all born the same.'

'Just as well. We could be like you.'

24

'No, I'm serious. You've got to be patient. He's away from his mum and dad.'

'It's not that.'

'What then?'

'I don't know.' Toby shrugged. 'I just don't like him, I suppose.'

Benjamin was coming back, apparently out of breath already, then, a few yards from them, he stopped, took off his glasses and pointed with them to where he had been standing.

'Where's that mist come from?'

Toby gave a start, both surprised and slightly disappointed that he hadn't spotted the grey cloud rolling up from the low ground towards them. Gordon stared at it too.

'Funny, I could have sworn that wasn't there a minute ago.'

Toby watched, uneasily: there was something about this mist that seemed unusual, and he was sure it hadn't been there when they arrived. He wondered how fast mist could travel.

Gordon dipped into the bucket-bag.

'Mist or no mist, I've got to sort out this fence. You two can disappear but don't go too far.'

'Where do you want to go?' said Benjamin.

'How should I know?' said Toby, turning away.

He wandered along the western fence, not looking to see whether Benjamin had followed but aware from the sound of laboured breathing that he was somewhere behind. No need to slow down or stop. He turned north and carried on as far as the plantation.

Benjamin caught him up breathlessly.

'I remember these trees, but they've grown a lot since last time. What are they called?'

'Sitka. Dad's little hobby. We'll probably need it, the way farming's going at the moment. He's got some larch too, back near the tractor. You wouldn't recognize 'em.'

25

'Sitka.' Benjamin's brow wrinkled. 'I remember, you told me last time.'

'*I* told you?'

'Yes, you were standing here—well, not here, over that way a bit—and you had a green jacket on. With a Manchester United badge on it.'

'Mum's thrown that away.'

'Oh.'

'It was falling apart. Anyway, I support Spurs now. Come on.'

He could see Benjamin wanted to rest, but mischief prompted him to move on, to see how much the boy could take. He pushed ahead between the rows of sitka, running his hand along the spiny branches, then after a few minutes he stopped and listened for the sound of breathing or the tramp of feet in the undergrowth behind him. Hearing neither, he turned.

Benjamin was some way behind, his head low, and walking more slowly than ever.

'Benjamin!' he shouted. 'You coming or what?'

Benjamin looked up, then, to Toby's amazement, raced towards him, half-stumbling over the uneven ground.

'What's the matter now?' he called, but Benjamin rushed straight past. Toby ran after him and grabbed him by the arm.

'What's up? Where are you going?'

Benjamin stared ahead, gulping in breath.

'That fence.' He pointed to the end of the plantation. 'What's on the other side?'

'Trees, more land.'

'But further on.'

Toby frowned. 'Dragon's Rock.'

So that was it, this thing about Dragon's Rock. Benjamin walked closer to the fence, still staring beyond it towards the trees.

'Maybe that's where the nice lady comes from.'

Toby snorted.

26

'There's only one person who hangs round Dragon's Rock, and she's—' He broke off. 'I'm going back to the tractor,' he said, and stomped off through the plantation.

Nice lady, nice lady. He was starting to hate Benjamin, not just dislike him. He thought of Flash and the soft fur he'd touched and cried over. And the woman he knew had caused his pain.

And now Benjamin.

Gordon was waiting for him by the tractor.

'Where's Benjamin?'

He nodded back towards the sitka plantation.

'In there somewhere.'

'You shouldn't have taken him up that way. You know why. You'd better go back and find him.'

But there was no need.

Benjamin had emerged from the rows of sitka and was picking his way slowly back, his eyes cast down to the ground, his hands passing back and forth a tiny object.

And as Toby watched, the idea came back to his mind.

The raven passed overhead a second time.

4

The floorboard creaked and Toby held his breath while he waited for the silence to settle; then gradually the quietness of the night crept round him again and he inched his way forward.

The darkness was no problem: the moon cast a cool light through the landing window and brightened the floor ahead. Down in the hall he heard the soft chime of the clock.

One o'clock.

He felt a chill round his neck and fastened the top button of his pyjamas, momentarily wondering why he was doing this. But doubts were brief; Benjamin deserved it and that was reason enough. Besides, he told himself, it was only for fun.

Benjamin's door was ajar, and that made things easier. He pushed it slowly.

And drew breath.

But it was only the glow of the moon on Benjamin's face that gave the eerie impression that he was awake. He crept forward and bent over the bed; Benjamin was lying on his back, a moon-halo round his head, weird and slightly unnerving. He glanced at the window, wishing the curtains had been drawn right across and that the moon were not so bright. The face below him looked harmless enough, yet there was still something unsettling about it. The mouth was open and the breathing so quiet it was hard to believe Benjamin was alive; only the slight movement of the chest betrayed it. He remembered watching Flash sleep.

The eyelids started to flicker.

Dreaming, he thought. He remembered Gordon saying

that when you blinked a lot it meant you were dreaming. Suddenly Benjamin moaned.

He took a step back, certain that someone in the house must have heard.

But no one stirred and Benjamin rolled over the other way. He waited a moment longer, then put his mind on what he had come to do. Benjamin's clothes lay on the seat at the foot of the bed, neatly folded, unlike his own. He crept over and felt through the pockets.

Nothing there. He looked round the room and saw the suitcase lying flat on the floor in the corner, tiptoed to it and bent down. To his relief the catches did not click as he opened it.

But the suitcase was empty.

Another moan from the bed made him look round. Benjamin had rolled back and was facing his way again; the eyelids still flickered and now from the mouth there came a strange, wordless murmuring.

Then he saw what he had come for.

In Benjamin's hand.

He stared in dismay. This was something he had never expected. Benjamin had pushed the sheets down slightly, and as Toby watched, he saw the hands move together and apart, together and apart, as though feeling along a string of beads.

But there were no beads.

Only the stone.

He watched, with a mixture of frustration and disbelief. It seemed impossible that Benjamin could sleep and yet pass the stone from hand to hand without dropping it.

Footsteps sounded outside the door.

Benjamin shifted restlessly, as though he had heard. Toby shrank back, trying to keep to the shadier part of the room in case Benjamin woke up. The footsteps made their way down to the bathroom. He listened, once again holding his breath. It sounded like Gordon, but he couldn't be sure.

For what seemed a long time he heard nothing, then the

29

footsteps returned, a door closed and silence fell once more. He looked quickly back at Benjamin. It was now or never.

For a moment something made him hesitate: the silent room, the shadows, the moon on the face; he didn't know. But the dare he had imposed upon himself was stronger.

Before he knew it, he had plucked the stone from Benjamin's fingers and was back at the door. With any luck he'd be able to slip out before Benjamin saw him. But, in spite of himself, he cast a quick glance back.

To his surprise, all was as before.

No change of position, no eyes upon him, no voice calling his name. Benjamin had not woken up.

And the hands passed back and forth an imaginary stone.

In the morning Benjamin was gone.

Toby kept quiet at the breakfast table and let the others argue it out.

'He must have been early,' Dad said. 'Gordon or I would have seen him if he'd gone out after six. I don't like this at all. It's very dark these mornings, he doesn't know his way about and he's a bit helpless.'

'But where would he go?' said Mum.

Gordon downed his tea.

'Toby took him up the sitka plantation yesterday.'

Toby saw Dad's mouth tighten.

'What did you go up there for, for God's sake?'

He shrugged. 'I don't know, just did.'

'How close to Dragon's Rock did you go?'

'Not very.'

'Close enough to see the buildings?'

'I'm not that stupid.'

'Over the boundary fence?'

'No.'

Dad frowned at him, then went over and started to lay

30

the fire. 'You're not being very helpful. Now think. Did he say anything or do anything that might give us a clue? Was he worried about anything? Interested in anything?'

Images started to mingle in Toby's mind: the mist below the fence, the raven; Benjamin staring.

'He seemed sort of worked up about Dragon's Rock. Wondered if it was the place where that "nice lady" lives.'

Dad dropped the kindling.

'Come on, Gordon.'

Toby jumped up. 'Can I come?'

'Not if we're going near Dragon's Rock.'

'More eyes the better, Dad,' said Gordon.

'All right, but no running off.'

'Promise.'

Mum hurried with them to the door.

'I'll stay here in case he wanders back on his own.'

The fields were bright and silvery with frost as the sun rose above them, fiery and gold. Toby jumped into the Land Rover and shivered on the cold seat; Dad climbed in the other side, slammed the door and started the engine. Gordon's face appeared at the window.

'I'll take the tractor down to the bottom fence. He might have gone down that way and had a fall or something. And there was a mist there yesterday. Meet you at the plantation.'

'Right,' said Dad. 'Let's go.'

5

Her face was hidden and she was bent over the ground, sorting with a billhook through a pile of long sticks she must have just cut from the forest nearby.

Benjamin crouched behind the fence at the top of the plantation, trying to keep out of sight just in case; then she turned slightly and he caught a glimpse of her face.

He relaxed.

It was all right after all. He'd been worried that it might have been the Wild Woman rather than the lady he'd seen the day he arrived, and for that brief moment, six years ago. So he hadn't been imagining it; she did exist. And now he had found her again, though he'd come out looking for something else.

She looked up suddenly and saw him.

He stiffened. 'I—'

At once she dropped the sticks and rushed away towards the trees.

'Wait!' he shouted.

She didn't turn, didn't stop.

'Wait!'

He climbed the fence and ran after her.

'I'm not going to hurt you!'

She hurried on, not looking back. He caught up with her but still she didn't slow down or look at him.

'Why are you frightened?' he said.

She flashed a glance at him, no more; but enough for him to catch the strange beauty of her eyes.

'You can't be scared of me,' he said. 'Nobody's ever scared of me.'

She stopped suddenly and peered at him hard, as though searching for some deception.

'What are you scared of?' he said.

Her eyes left him and darted about her. He followed them, trying to find a clue among the trees, bushes, and fields. A question rose in his mind, though why it came, he didn't know.

'Is it the Wild Woman you're scared of?'

Her eyes fixed on him again. 'What do you know about the Wild Woman?'

Her voice startled him: he had expected something hesitant, but this was deep and attractive. He tried, without much success, to make his own deep and attractive too.

'I only know what Toby's family told me. So it is the Wild Woman you're frightened of?'

She looked away again.

'Everybody's frightened of the Wild Woman. No one more so than me.'

'Is she so terrible?'

'Ask your friends. Ask anyone round here. They'll tell you what she's like.'

'But why are you more frightened of her than anyone else?'

'I'm her prisoner.'

She turned from him again, this time back to where she had left the sticks. He followed, glad that she seemed to trust him enough to speak; but surprised at what she had said. He remembered his purpose in coming out and wondered whether this meeting might be a part of that purpose. A part he had not foreseen.

'What's your name?' he said.

'Ione.'

She didn't ask his.

'Mine's Benjamin,' he said.

She reached the sticks and started to gather them, and he bent down to help. But she waved him aside.

'I don't need any favours.'

There was no anger in her voice; no sharpness.

Only pride.

But it was a tired pride, a pride he sensed had been tested, perhaps many times.

'What are the sticks for?' he said. 'To make a fire?'

'To make a cage. My cage.'

He stood back, unsure what to do or say. She seemed so capable, yet so vulnerable, and she said such strange things. He tried to guess how old she was but even that was hard to tell: older than Mum certainly, or Toby's mum, but not all shrivelled up like Aunty Maud.

The more he thought about her, the more mysterious she became.

'Why do you have to make a cage for yourself?'

She stood up, her arms clasped round the sticks.

'The Wild Woman forces me. I told you, I'm her prisoner. She's got a halter round my neck.'

'I can't see one.'

'No one can see it. But it's always there.'

'Can't you run away somewhere she can't get you?'

She gazed down the field, then, still holding the sticks, walked to the fence and looked over one of the sitka, its branches laced with gossamer.

'If the spider spins a strong web, you never escape.'

'But can't you go where there isn't a web?'

She set off back towards the trees.

'Not if it covers the whole world.'

He followed again, more and more drawn to her.

'Why haven't Toby's family seen you?'

'Nobody sees me.'

'But I see you.'

'You're different.'

Her face had lost its earlier agitation, but fear still hovered over the features like a shadow. He wondered what she meant about him being different.

'Why don't other people see you?' he said. 'Do you hide from them?'

She didn't answer. But he remembered how she ran away when she first saw him.

'Why do you hide?' he said. 'Please tell me.'

She threw him another glance, as brief as before.

'I'm an empath,' she said.

'An . . . empath?' He stared at her. 'What's an empath?'

She walked for a while in silence and he began to think she was not going to answer; then she began to speak.

'Some people have to live apart. They're too sensitive. They have too much empathy with the suffering of others. They feel the pain of the world as though it's their own, and it's too much to bear.'

'And are you . . . sensitive like that?'

She stopped and faced him.

'Go back to your friends. You shouldn't be out here.' She looked him over. 'You haven't even got a coat on.'

'I don't need one. I feel hot. Anyway, you haven't got a coat on either.'

Strange that he hadn't noticed it before. He had been so fascinated by her features that he hadn't realized she was wearing no coat. And what clothes she had were ragged: a tattered jumper, an equally tattered skirt, an apron made from what looked like sacking, and an old pair of worn-out boots.

Yet in a curious way, these things only highlighted the strange dignity in her face.

She said nothing in reply.

'Ione?' he said. It felt odd saying her name when he had only known her for a few minutes. 'What's the Wild Woman doing to you?'

'Destroying me,' she said. She nodded in the direction of the farm. 'Go back to your friends and don't come here again.'

'But I've got to. I've got to find the stone and put it back on the rock.'

'What stone?'

'When I was eight we came to stay at the farm. My

35

parents and Toby's parents all went to the same school and they're friends. Toby and I had to go out and play together. We came to the sitka plantation and Toby ran off, on purpose, and left me to find my own way home.'

He remembered Toby's face, scowling at him all through that first visit; just as it seemed to have scowled at him ever since.

'Toby hates me,' he said. 'I tried to get back by going through the forest but I got lost and found myself at this big rock. Down in a valley.'

He paused.

'It had some jagged bits and I put my feet on them. I don't know why but I just felt I wanted to climb it, to see if I could get to the top. I found a stone there, inside a little hole. It fitted perfectly, like a key.'

She said nothing but he sensed she was listening and went on.

'I took it. I collect stones and this was a lovely violet-coloured one. But I didn't show it to anyone. I kept it secret. I sort of knew I'd done something wrong. And that's when the nightmares started.'

A robin fluttered down to the ground, the brightness of its chest in cheerful contrast to the grey of the morning. Grasping the sticks tightly under one arm, she held out the billhook towards it. He waited for it to fly off.

To his surprise it hopped straight onto the blade, up her arm to the shoulder and down onto the sticks. She watched it for a moment, then looked at him again.

'What nightmares?' she said.

He took his eye from the robin and looked away over the fields.

'About a dragon,' he said. 'It's so scary. Ever since I took the stone, I've been having these nightmares. It's always the same one. I even had it on the train coming here. Mum and Dad have been worried sick about me. I know I should have come back before now to return the stone. But we've moved about so much, it hasn't been possible, and anyway,

I didn't want to have to put up with Toby again. And . . . and I suppose I sort of hoped the nightmares would go away and I could keep the stone. But they've just got worse.'

'What happens in the nightmare?'

'I'm being chased by this huge dragon, and it's getting closer and closer and closer, and any moment it's going to catch me. I can hear it roaring and feel its breath, but I never see its face. I always wake up just before I see it.' He found himself searching the landscape. 'And now I've got this feeling it's more than just a dream.'

'What do you mean?' she said.

He turned back to her and saw the robin still perched on the sticks.

'Toby's family told me the rock's called Dragon's Rock. I didn't know that before. And . . . ' He hesitated, unsure of whether he should tell her more. But she was still watching him, and seemed concerned about what he was saying. 'And I've just got this feeling the dragon's real. I can feel it, somewhere close, somewhere really close. But I can't see it and I'm frightened. And . . . and I feel so hot all the time.' He looked at her sharply. 'You haven't got a coat on. Is that 'cause you feel hot too?'

She turned towards the trees and the robin flew off.

'Go home,' she said. 'And when you find the stone, give it back to the rock.'

'But I might not find it.'

'Maybe your friend's taken it.'

He pondered this, remembering Toby's malicious interest in the stone during the tractor ride. He'd been thinking he must have dropped it, but Toby . . .

It was certainly possible.

She had started to walk away again, back to the forest, to her hidden life, her fears, her cage. Her empathy with the world. And he knew that this time she would not let him follow. But one problem still bothered him, though why he felt she might be able to explain it was a mystery to him.

Perhaps because she hadn't answered his last question.

'Ione, why do I feel hot all the time?'

She stopped and half-turned towards him.

'Because the dragon's angry,' she said.

'So there is a dragon!' He stepped forward eagerly. 'But where is it? What does it look like?'

She motioned him back.

'You must find that out for yourself.'

'But is it my fault?' he said, searching her face. 'That it's angry, I mean.'

She looked him over for a few moments, as though trying to decide whether to respond; then slowly nodded. And before he could speak again, she walked quickly on and disappeared among the trees.

From below the plantation he heard the sound of the Land Rover.

6

Benjamin slept through the rest of the morning.

When he came downstairs in the early afternoon, Toby noticed he was withdrawn and uncommunicative. Not that he cared. For him Benjamin was a source of nothing but contempt: not a word about why he'd gone running out, just a lot of rubbish about meeting the 'nice lady'.

There was only one woman roaming these parts.

And everyone knew what she was like.

He remembered the drive that morning across the frosty landscape, the strange mist creeping up from the lower fields as they scoured the ground; and how he'd spotted her, just for a second, through the back of the Land Rover as they headed for home with Benjamin, her face dark against the sky.

And how the darkness remained, even after she'd turned away.

Lunch was a depressing affair, and it didn't help to see the others trying to act natural, as though nothing were wrong. Presumably he was meant to do the same.

Well, he wouldn't. Benjamin was a liar and running away was just a sympathy act to get attention, which obviously had worked. He heard his name mentioned and saw Dad looking at him.

'We thought you might like to take Benjamin round with you this afternoon.'

It didn't take much in the way of brains to work out why. But the prospect of an afternoon with Benjamin was too much. He tried to think of a way out. 'I'm not really going anywhere. I was going to finish some whittling.'

'Yes, but . . . you know . . . ' He heard a touch of exasperation in Dad's voice. 'You could take him round a bit, show him some of your secret haunts.'

'What secret haunts?'

'Well, places you go to get away from us lot.'

He could see there was no point in arguing, as Dad's mind was obviously made up.

Suddenly Benjamin spoke.

'Maybe we could go back to that field. The one you found me in.'

Toby looked round for reactions but the others were clearly determined to appear normal. Dad even put a napkin to his mouth, something he never did.

'Back to Skinny Sam?' he said. 'Well, I'd prefer it if you went somewhere—'

'Skinny Sam?' Benjamin leaned forward. 'Who's Skinny Sam?'

Gordon laughed.

'Skinny Sam's the field. Thought you knew. We give all our fields names. Skinny Sam's the one I took you to yesterday, just below the sitka. Where Toby and Dad found you this morning.'

'But why Skinny Sam?'

'Can't you guess?'

'Because it's skinny?'

Toby sighed. Bravo. And he could guess the next question.

'What do you call the other fields?'

Spot on. Ten out of ten.

Dad reached for his tobacco pouch.

'Paddy's Pasture.' He pointed with his pipe out of the window. 'That's the one out there. Then you've got Norman's Nook, Dawny's Dip, Ivan's Meadow, Lizzie's Hollow.'

'Molly the Twist,' said Gordon. 'Long Louis, Big Willy.'

'Big Willy?' Benjamin tittered. 'Have you really got a field called Big Willy?'

'What's wrong with that?' said Toby.

But the others were laughing too and nobody took any notice of him.

'It's sort of a funny shape,' explained Gordon. 'If you know what I mean.'

Mum began to collect the plates.

'The fields had other names when we moved here but we decided to give them our own private ones.'

'What for?' said Benjamin.

'We didn't like the old ones. Each field's got its own personality. So we made up our own names, based on eccentric characters we've known over the years and what each field's like.'

'Mucky Meg,' offered Gordon.

Benjamin looked round at him.

'Mucky Meg?'

'Where Mum lost her boots.'

Benjamin's face clouded again.

'It's very muddy,' said Toby testily. 'And Mum's name's Meg.'

He wondered how much longer they were going to humour the idiot, with his pathetic questions and nervous nodding gestures. And the movements, seemingly unconscious, of the fingers.

Those he liked least of all.

He remembered the way the fingers had moved as the moonlight played on the face; as he waited and watched in the night. And he felt a sudden urge to run upstairs and check under his pillow.

Benjamin gazed dreamily out of the window.

'This land, it's . . . it's so strange now.'

'Strange?' said Mum. 'In what way?'

'It was different last time.' Benjamin frowned. 'It seemed all velvety then but now it's—'

He stopped, and seemed to be searching for the right word.

'It's what?' said Mum.

41

'Sort of scaly,' he said finally. The wispy hair fell across his face and he pushed it back.

'Scaly!' said Mum. 'I've not heard it called that before.'

'It's like a dragon's body,' said Benjamin. 'A big dragon, lying asleep. But starting to wake up.'

She laughed. 'The things you think of. Anyway, what about doing the Christmas tree? We could—' She broke off suddenly. 'Are you all right, Benjamin?'

Benjamin was suddenly breathing heavily.

'I'm . . . so hot,' he said.

She rested a hand on his arm.

'You've been up half the night, running about the fields without a coat on. You've probably picked up something.'

'I'm still ever so tired.'

'Well, why don't you go back to bed for the afternoon? I'll come and wake you in time for supper.'

'Can I?'

'Of course. We'll see if you still feel hot when you wake up. Come on.'

Toby glared after them as they left the room, and heard his thoughts mimic Benjamin's voice.

I'm . . . so hot. I'm still ever so tired.

Only Benjamin could feel hot when it was freezing cold, and if he was tired, that was his fault.

And scaly! Like a dragon's body!

'What a twit,' he muttered and walked out into the yard. The animals stirred restlessly around him.

Benjamin did not appear for supper.

But he was there. Toby could see from the others' faces that even from upstairs Benjamin could intrude upon everyone's thoughts.

After supper they took their tea through to the living-room. Toby sat at the end of the sofa, watching the flames from the fire flicker round the wall. For some reason he still felt cold and the room seemed dark, despite the glow from the hearth and the big lamp in the corner. He stood up and switched on the main light. Dad blinked and rubbed his eyes.

'Turn that off. I was dozing.'

'Sorry,' he said and switched it off again.

'I'll pop up and see how Benjamin is,' said Mum.

He listened to the sound of her footsteps on the stairs, then above his head as she walked across the landing. All of a sudden the room seemed darker, colder. He threw another log on the fire and stretched towards it, listening to the steady crackle of burning wood.

Footsteps sounded on the stair again, then Mum burst into the room.

'Quick! Benjamin's rolling about the bed. Mumbling something. I can't wake him.'

The others rushed on ahead, and Toby hurried after them. But at the top of the stairs he stopped.

Through the open door of Benjamin's room he could hear Mum's voice, coaxing, encouraging. He waited a few seconds to make sure no one was coming out, then turned towards his own room.

It was no good; he had to see the stone, had to make sure it was still there. He didn't know why it mattered so much, or why he had to check it now. But that was the way it was. He pushed open the door.

And stood back in disbelief.

The wardrobe doors were open and the drawers had been pulled out from the chest and desk. His jacket had been thrown over the chair and he knew he had left it hanging on the door.

Benjamin.

It could only be Benjamin. So obsessed that he hadn't even bothered to tidy up and pretend he hadn't been there. And there was only one thing he could have been looking for. He ran to the bed and lifted the pillow.

The stone seemed to stare up at him accusingly.

He heard footsteps outside and hurriedly replaced the

pillow. A moment later Mum appeared in the doorway. He shifted from one foot to the other, disconcerted by her expression.

'Is Benjamin all right?' he said.

She walked slowly into the room, looking about her.

'What was Benjamin trying to find in here?'

'I don't know. Has he woken up?'

'What was he looking for?'

'How do you know he's been in here?'

'He just told me.'

'Well, he must have told you what he was looking for, then.'

'He said it's a secret but I have a feeling you know what it is.'

Gordon's voice boomed out from down the corridor.

'Mum, can you come back?'

She looked at him hard for a moment, but then turned and left. He followed surlily, hearing now from Benjamin's room the voice he had come to despise. He stopped in the doorway and looked in.

Dad and Gordon stood by the window; Mum sat on the bed, leaning forward; and Benjamin was holding her hand.

'A big dragon,' he was saying, 'a great big dragon . . . '

Toby stepped in and Benjamin looked up. And the two of them stared at each other without speaking.

'Toby,' said Mum, 'did you put the guard across the fire before you came up?'

'No.'

'Can you go down and do it now?'

He lingered, unwilling to stay, yet more unwilling to go back to the strange chill of the living-room.

'What's all this stuff about a dragon?' he said.

'Never mind,' she said. 'It's a nightmare Benjamin keeps having.'

'About a dragon?'

'Yes, a big dragon. Now will you go and sort out the fire?'

He looked at Gordon and Dad, wishing one of them

would say something to keep him there, but neither spoke. He made his way slowly back to the living-room.

A shiver ran through him as he entered, though he didn't know why. He stood close to the door, watching the shadows above the fire ripple over the wall like barley swaying in a field. This was stupid, he told himself; he'd lived in the house all his life and never felt scared before. He walked to the centre of the room.

It was all Benjamin's fault. Ever since he'd turned up, things hadn't been right, and here he was again pretending he was having some crazy nightmare about a dragon, just to get more attention. The others were stupid to take him so seriously. He walked closer to the fire but the warmth did not increase.

Steps sounded on the stairs again and the others came back in, fortunately without Benjamin. He waited to see whether anyone would say something about the change in the atmosphere.

Gordon stood over the fire and rubbed his hands; Dad threw himself in the armchair.

'Right, Toby,' he said. 'What was Benjamin looking for in your room?'

'I don't know.'

'So why would he go and hunt through your things?'

'Don't ask me.'

He saw Mum walking round the room, looking about her.

'What's up, Mum?' said Gordon.

'I thought I heard something.'

She stopped walking and looked at Toby.

'Toby, if you have taken something of Benjamin's—'

'I haven't.'

'If you have,' she said firmly, 'you must give it back.'

She listened again. Dad sat up.

'What is it?'

'I'm sure I heard something.'

'The animals?'

'Sssh!'

Talking ceased and now Toby began to feel the unearthly stillness in the house, broken only by the crackle of the fire and the occasional squeak of the chair springs as Dad shifted his weight. Something clipped the windowpane: a branch from the apple tree perhaps, caught in the breeze, but Toby jumped all the same. Now, more than ever, he wanted someone to say something, anything, just to break the silence. He wanted someone to put the main light on.

But no one spoke and no one moved.

The glow from the lamp seemed weird and wan and oddly interwoven with the tiny figures of shadow thrown up from the fire onto the wall. And as Toby watched them, he felt the darkness and coldness deepen around him, and the certainty came that this silent room now housed a sinister intelligence.

A spark flew from the fire and landed on the carpet. Gordon reached down and flicked it onto the tiles.

The back door clicked and footsteps sounded on the gravel.

Running.

Dad jumped up.

'Quick!' he said and ran out of the room, closely followed by Gordon. Toby made for the door too.

But Mum barred his way.

'Toby, there's nothing you want to tell me, is there?'

He bit his lip, then shook his head.

'No, Mum,' he said, and raced past her towards the back door.

7

Benjamin heard them calling.

But he took no notice and ran on down the slushy path by the paddock as far as the gate. Only then did he stop and listen for sounds of pursuit.

Toby's father was still shouting after him, but there were no footsteps yet. Probably they would take the Land Rover like last time. He climbed the gate and ran across the field.

The voices grew more distant and eventually died away. He slowed down and tried to decide which way to go. Last night he had run without thinking, and found his way to Skinny Sam and the sitka plantation more by accident than skill.

Tonight must be different.

Tonight he had to go further, to continue the search, not just for the stone this time, because he was starting to have a suspicion about who might have that, but for the other things that had haunted him for the last six years.

He looked about him, wishing there were more moonlight to see by. Yet curiously there was some light: a light he had seen last night as he raced over the fields, a strange luminosity that seemed to issue from the ground itself. As though the soil were breathing, like the body of an animal.

Sleeping.

But restless.

He walked on, treading carefully, anxious not to disturb this terrifying beast. He was feeling hot again, and he knew it wasn't fever but the suffocating closeness that had afflicted him since his first trip to Devon. Thoughts of the dragon began to pour through his mind again, and as he looked over the land, he began to sense a new, bestial form.

He came to a fence, climbed over it and found himself among gorse and long grass. Nothing here seemed familiar. He tried to remember the way he had to go, but the distant memory in his mind was only of the destination.

He looked towards what he thought was the south. If this was the right way, Skinny Sam and the plantation must be below him somewhere to the left. He tried to remember the name of the field he had just crossed.

Mucky Meg.

That was it, the muddy one. He remembered Toby's scornful expression when he'd explained why they called it that. But this wasn't the time to think of Toby. He had to keep his wits about him if he was to find what he was looking for.

And avoid the person he feared.

He thought of what the others had said about the Wild Woman, and what Ione had said; and he found himself looking about him as he walked.

Ione.

If only he could speak to her again. There was something so fascinating, so mysterious about her, so—

He stopped suddenly, convinced he was being watched.

He didn't know why he thought that. Maybe it was the inner sense he had come to rely on over the years. But in the silent landscape of bushes and long grass, he sensed an attentive presence.

A whine cut through the night.

He tensed, wondering what it was, and where.

The ground still exuded a ghostly light, and the bushes and hillocks and swaying grass seemed sombre and hostile. He looked over his shoulder, trying to work out where the farm was. And he realized he was lost.

The whine came again, closer. He looked quickly about

him, straining to catch a moving shape among the shadowy forms.

There, to the left. Or maybe—

He turned and scanned the dark clumps of gorse, and his boot sank into a patch of slush. The whine came again, and with it a scurrying sound.

Then silence.

He was more frightened than ever now. Frightened of going on and frightened of going back. And frightened of this glistening land on which he stood.

His other boot was sinking too. He pulled them both out and forced himself to walk on. There was nothing else for it. He had to find the place again, even if he couldn't complete the task he had come back to fulfil.

He plodded on, hoping he was heading west, and gradually the ground became firmer, though still it was unfamiliar. He had been hoping to cut across north of the sitka plantation and perhaps come upon something he remembered, but there was nothing here that he recognized. Certainly he hadn't come this way last night when he ran out and groped his way up from Skinny Sam, or that first time all those years ago.

But perhaps he had come this way: parts of it felt peculiarly familiar, as though the land were a huge serpent that had simply changed its skin. He came to a fence and climbed over and the moment he did so, he knew he had been here before.

He found himself thinking of Ione again, and wondered where she was right now. Sleeping safe, he hoped, even though she was in a cage. He walked a little faster, trying to blot from his mind the thought of the other person who roamed these lands.

This person wouldn't be sleeping, of that he was sure. Probably she never slept; probably she roamed through the nights like a phantom, maybe even watching him this very minute. She wouldn't fear the world like Ione; it was obviously the world that feared her.

He stopped at another patch of gorse, breathing hard. He had never liked exercise, even walking, and always had his leg pulled by the other boys when they had games. He picked his way through the gorse and bracken, and the ground started to soften again. He stared about him, trying to decide which way to go next.

And the landscape seemed to stare back, as though waiting to see what he would do.

Turn right, he told himself. Try north. If that's where north is.

Immediately the land felt more comfortable: there were fewer bushes and shrubs here, and the ground seemed firmer. After a while he saw trees ahead. The land was climbing too, leaving behind the flat, slushy ground he had come through. He walked on for a few minutes, then tripped and fell, face-down, into a small hollow.

Spitting earth from his mouth, he scrambled to the farther edge and looked out. And to his surprise found that the ground fell away into a small valley.

Stretching round the top he saw trees moving against the sky. Beyond them, the skeleton of a house.

The roofless shell that housed no one but had dwelt in his mind ever since he first saw it six years ago.

And below the house, at the bottom of the valley: the rock.

He gazed at it, memories pouring back. Somehow, now that he was here, he felt unwilling to approach. He looked about, searching for danger, then cautiously made his way down. A few feet away, he stopped: it seemed smaller than he remembered, though it was still twice his size. But he had been smaller when he first came, he thought, so perhaps that was the reason.

Then, as he stood there, a feeling of its vastness came back, a feeling that the rock was but an acorn, yet he could sense an oak. He wanted to touch it, but didn't dare.

He walked round it, studying it from all sides, searching in the darkness for the features he had seen in his memory.

And as he walked, it seemed that the rock grew and grew until it dominated the valley.

He heard a rustling sound up the slope.

But all he saw was the ruin rising above him.

He moved closer to the rock and now he saw that, like the ground, it too had a luminosity. And as he drew closer still, he began to feel the heat, just as he had felt it that first time, and ever since, no matter where he was. Yet here it was more intense, more enticing, more frightening.

Unable to resist any longer, he reached out and touched the surface. Surprisingly it was cool, but as he moved his palm upwards, the body of the rock grew hotter. He paused, allowing the strange energy to run through his arm and into his body; and the little stone came back to his mind.

What made him look up the slope again he didn't know. It wasn't a sound or scent or movement in the corner of his eye. But with a sureness that tensed his whole body, he knew someone was near.

He backed away from the rock and crouched behind a bush, searching anxiously about him. Nothing seemed different but the valley had begun to emanate a new presence.

He heard the snap of a twig, then the soft sucking sound of footsteps in wet ground. He stiffened, trying to gauge where they were coming from. But it was impossible. One moment they seemed to be behind him, then to his right, then to his left.

Finally he saw.

A woman was standing by the rock. He didn't know how she had come, whether down the slope from the ruin, or by some other way. But he knew enough.

It was the person he dreaded most in all the world.

As though sensing him, she twisted and stared towards the bush. He held his breath, fighting the urge to call out. Her features were hidden in the darkness but he felt the power in her face, the strength in her body.

51

She began to circle the rock, running her hand over the surface, just as he had done only moments ago. He watched and shuddered. Her body seemed as lithe as a cat, as strong as a bear, and it oozed menace. He thought of Ione, gentle, frightened Ione, and knew she would be powerless against this woman.

This woman could do anything she wanted. The dread of discovery churned his stomach into a knot of fear. With that dread came the conviction that she knew he was there, that she was playing with him, letting him suffer before catching him.

And she would catch him. He knew he could not outrun her.

And what she would do with him he did not dare to think.

But it was not the strength of her body that frightened him most. It was the dark power that swirled about her like a river, a power he knew was harnessed to the rock. A power that now harnessed him.

The whine he had heard earlier split the silence again.

The woman took her hand from the rock and sniffed the air, then, to his relief, began to climb the slope towards the ruin.

He edged round, ready to run.

At once she turned and looked back towards him.

He froze, certain that now he had been seen. She stood motionless, still staring towards the bush behind which he crouched, and for a moment he saw the gleam of an eye in that dark, featureless face. Then she turned back up the slope and disappeared among the trees.

The moment she was gone, he buried himself in flight.

He had never run like this before, even when he escaped from the farm. Heat still licked about him. His head started to spin. He knew he had to keep calm or he would never find the way back.

But his mind was racing too. And as he ran he thought of the Wild Woman. Maybe she was close behind him. Maybe she didn't go back to the ruin. Maybe she turned right at the top of the valley.

She could reappear any moment.

Behind. In front.

Anywhere.

And she would kill him.

With one hand. Or just a look.

He plunged into a brook and out the other side, dimly aware that he hadn't passed it on the way out. A fence appeared before him. He scrambled over it and found himself among trees. Gasping for breath, he drew up, trying to force himself to think of where he was.

But his mind would not think. His mind said 'run'.

The whine broke through the night again. He whirled round, expecting to see the Wild Woman's eyes burning into his own.

He saw no face, no eyes. Only the grizzled countenances of trees. Yet he felt her presence, everywhere.

The whine came again.

He tore into the forest. Branches seemed to swing out, clutching, clasping, clinging. He broke through them, his glasses almost falling from his eyes. Now he saw her face, staring from every tree, every tussock, every rock, and from the spectral darkness that seeped around him like a cloud.

He started to shout, and shout, and shout.

A figure loomed in front of him.

8

'I found him at the bottom end of the forest,' said Gordon.

He looked wearily at Benjamin, fast asleep in the corner of the kitchen by the stove.

'He was out of his mind, shouting his head off. Just as well probably, I might not have found him otherwise. He didn't know what was going on. I called his name and he bolted the other way. I had to run and catch him.'

Toby looked at his parents, both still in their coats like Gordon and himself, and just as bleary-eyed; and he wondered how popular Benjamin was now. Dad glanced balefully at his watch.

'Three o'bloody clock in the morning, and two nights in a row. What's he up to, for God's sake?' He looked at Gordon. 'Did he say anything about what he'd been doing?'

'Don't think he even recognized me. He was scared out of his mind. I just bundled him into the Land Rover.'

Mum sighed.

'I'm really bothered about this. I hate to think of him wandering round Dragon's Rock.'

Toby fumbled with his gloves, still wondering when somebody would mention the chilly atmosphere in the house. Maybe the others had hoped it would go away while they were out looking for Benjamin, but they must have noticed it; it was even worse than yesterday.

And it had spread.

He glowered at the floor. All this had happened since Benjamin came to stay: the coldness in the house, all the talk about the nice lady he claimed he'd seen, and dragons, and running off.

And the stone.

And Flash, dear old Flash. He thought of the dog as he'd been before Benjamin came, healthy and sleek, lying on the grass, ready for work or fun. Then as Gordon had found him, the fur ruffled and pricked where the crows had been.

And the eyes. Toby gulped. He remembered the eyes.

Dad yawned.

'Whatever's going on, we'll have to have a talk with Benjamin, when he's had some rest. Talking of which—'

'Dad?' said Toby. 'What are we going to do about the house?'

It was obvious the others were avoiding the matter for some reason, so he would have to bring it up himself.

'What's wrong with the house?' said Dad.

'You know what I mean. It's cold.'

'We've still got to sleep.'

'But there's a . . . funny atmosphere as well.'

'I'm too tired to notice anything at the moment.'

Gordon rubbed his eyes.

'Sleep in my room if you want, Toby. I can probably put up with your snoring for what's left of the night.'

'No, thanks.'

'Sure, Toby?' said Dad. 'Sounds like a good idea, if you're worried.'

'I'm not worried. It's OK. No problem.'

He looked quickly away; this wasn't the time to show anyone he was frightened. And now he was puzzled too. They must have noticed the atmosphere; it couldn't just be him.

'What about Benjamin?' said Mum. 'If anyone needs company, he does. If only to keep an eye on him.'

'No need to worry about Benjamin,' said Gordon. He nodded towards the stove. 'He's out for the count.'

Dad stood up.

'Let's get some sleep. We'll see how Benjamin is at breakfast and try and get him to tell us what he was up to.'

'It might be an idea to get him away from the farm for a

few hours,' said Mum. 'Give him a change of scene.'

'I've got to go into Totnes,' said Gordon.

'Fine,' said Dad. 'Take the boys with you. Now let's go to bed.'

'And Toby,' said Mum, 'you're to come to our room if you feel frightened.'

'I'm not frightened.'

'No, of course you're not.'

Gordon walked over to the stove where Benjamin was slumped in the chair, still fast asleep.

'Might as well carry him. He's not going to wake up.'

They hung up their coats and Dad led the way out of the room, Toby following, Mum close behind and Gordon at the rear, the sleeping Benjamin in his arms. For Toby the relative cheer of the kitchen vanished as they entered the hall and the chill he had felt seeping into the kitchen enveloped him like a fog. He shivered and found himself wanting to look round at Mum and Gordon; but he kept his eyes on Dad's back and walked on, across the hall and up the stairs.

And as he climbed, he felt the coldness move with him.

Dad stopped at the top of the stairs and the others crowded round him.

'You're still looking worried, Toby,' he said. 'Want me to leave the landing light on?'

Toby tried to look unconcerned.

'Don't mind. Could do.'

'Leave it on,' said Gordon. 'I'll put Benjamin to bed. Toby, come into my room if you change your mind.'

'Or ours,' said Mum. 'And leave your bedside light on if you want to.'

'I'm OK, Mum. I told you.'

'All right,' she said and kissed him. 'Goodnight, then.'

'Goodnight.'

He entered his room, switched on the light, and closed the door behind him. And as he'd feared, the coldness slid after him.

He sat on the bed, knowing he would not sleep, and that he had several hours to endure before it would be light enough to go out and do what he had decided he must do. It would have been better done now, in the darkness, away from prying eyes, but the darkness was too frightening, especially outside on his own, even among the fields he knew so well.

He looked about him, wondering how familiar things could possibly have become so threatening since Benjamin came.

Benjamin, bloody Benjamin.

For a moment fear fell back as anger rose within him. He held on to it, determined not to lose it, and tried to think what to do for the next few hours. The urge to reach under the pillow was strong but he checked himself; somehow he knew that the presence in the house and in this very room was linked to that tiny thing he had prized, but which now weighed like a colossal burden upon him. He reached instead for the stump he'd found the week before Benjamin came.

Benjamin. Anger. Hold on to it.

He rummaged in the drawer of the cabinet and pulled out his favourite whittling knife.

Hold on to the anger. Use it.

He turned the stump and examined it, remembering the dog's glee on finding it at the foot of the privet. Dear old Flash. More anger flooded in and he struck out with the knife. Before long chips were flying over the floor.

'Some kind of reptile, that's what you'll be.'

He plucked away a couple of strands with his blade and took a shaving from the curved top.

'Hang on, we'll leave you as you are up here. Then you can be holding something in your mouth.'

He trimmed the lower part of the stump and gradually it took shape: a slender body, curving upwards from the belly, the head back, and some large object in its mouth.

'Your prey,' he said. 'What'll it be?'

He pondered this for a while, idly stroking the wood with the flat of the blade.

'You can be a dragon,' he said suddenly. 'Seeing as Benjamin keeps having nightmares about a dragon, or so he says. And your prey . . . '

He smiled; he knew what the prey would be.

Now the blade was rasping over the wood, chipping, shaping, refining. He smiled again: no one else would recognize the prey, but he would always know what it was. He glared round the room at the unseen presence.

'You haven't stopped me whittling, whatever you are. You haven't—'

A wailing call sounded in the night. He clutched the dragon to him and listened. A moment later it came again, an eerie, plaintive cry, just outside the window. Gripping the dragon tightly, he turned off the light and peered out.

At first all was blackness outside and he could see nothing; then, little by little, the darkness softened. Just below him, on one of the new fence posts, was a large black shape. It seemed somehow hooded or arched over, its back flexed into a curve so perfect it seemed sculptured in stillness; then it twisted its head and two eyes flashed up at him.

It was a cat.

But that made him feel no better. There weren't any cats round here. None on the farm because of Mum's allergy, and the nearest local cat was over at Brambles Farm and much too decrepit to drag itself here.

And this was no ordinary stray. There was something about the way it moved its head, the way it crouched and twisted its body, the way it looked up, aware of him.

Suddenly it tensed. The eyes blinked, the back lengthened, it reared on its haunches, its head high; and once more the call broke the silence of the night.

He started to open the window.

'I don't think I like the look of you.'

Unhurriedly the creature stretched out its paws and

clawed the edge of the post, then the long shape tightened and quivered, the face turned, and the eyes glinted up at him again.

The next moment it was gone.

He fastened the window again and sat on the edge of the bed, thinking of the cat, and the chill in the house, and what he had to do. And as he sat and shivered and trembled, he gazed out of the window at the slow, cold lightening of the sky.

9

At dawn, he was out.

No need to tell anyone anything.

Just get it over and done with.

He ran round the house, hoping no one had heard him leave. The curtains were drawn but he doubted whether anyone had slept well. And Dad and Gordon were always up early.

No time to waste. The breeze was bracing but he was glad of it; it forced away the hunger for sleep. And the sky was reassuringly bright and clear after the shadowy turmoil of the night. He noticed that the coldness of the house had followed him.

Never mind that now, he thought. First things first. He stole round the side of the house, listening for sounds behind Gordon's window. But all was silent. He crept over to the shrubbery fence, looked up at his own window, then down at the posts.

That was the one, third from the end. He walked over and examined it but there was no sign of fur or scratch marks, not that he'd expected any. The animal was probably miles away by now. He turned back towards the yard.

And gave a start.

Up in the silver birch was a large black form. But it was not a cat.

It was a raven.

Or rather, *the* raven: he knew it was the one he'd spotted at Skinny Sam the time they took Benjamin out in the tractor. He'd seen plenty of ravens up on the moor but never in this part of Devon before. But that wasn't the only reason why he recognized it.

This raven was awesomely large.

He walked across the yard, leaned on the paddock gate and looked up at the bird sitting motionless above him.

'There's something about you I don't trust,' he murmured.

As though it had understood him, the bird flapped off the branch and swung away over Long Louis. He watched it disappear, then hurried down the path towards Mucky Meg.

Nothing else matters so long as it's done.

He pulled the overcoat tight around him and knotted the scarf a second time. The sky seemed to be losing its brightness already and suddenly looked grey and menacing; and the air was growing colder still. He heard a gruff croaking sound behind him and looked back at the house.

There was the raven again, this time waddling round the rim of the chimney. He walked quickly on down the track until he reached the gate into Mucky Meg. The wood was damp but he climbed astride and sat there to look out over the field. But the field was no longer there to see.

It had been swallowed in mist.

His mouth dropped open and he stared about him.

To the left, Long Louis was still clear and so were the fields to the south-east, but the whole of the forest to the west was gone, even the tops of the trees. He looked north towards the lane: that was clear, and he could see all the way along the hedge to the end, and into Big Willy. He gazed back at Mucky Meg and saw smudges of mist rolling in bulbous clouds from the south and west like an incoming tide.

But the job still had to be done. He jumped down from the gate into the slush. The mist'll even help, he thought, and reached into his pocket.

Cruk! Cruk! Cruk!

Startled, he looked up.

61

A hundred feet up he saw the raven soaring. After a while it stopped and hung there, directly above him, spiralling in the currents, then it swooped down over the field again and vanished in the mist. He glared after it and pulled out the stone.

It seemed to sparkle in the light and felt warm in his hand. He played with it for a moment, stroking the sides, then running his finger over the hardness of the base.

'Two-faced,' he said. 'That's what you are. One side nice and smooth. The other side you'll cut me.'

He tossed and caught it a couple of times.

'And there's been nothing but trouble since he brought you.'

He gazed out at the misty visage of Mucky Meg, closed his fingers round the stone and crooked his arm back for the throw.

Cruk! Cruk! Cruk!

Again the black speck appeared, soaring and circling, in and out of the mist. He relaxed his arm; there was something unsettling about this bird, and not just the fact that it was so big. He threw his arm back again.

Cruk! Cruk! Cruk!

Again the gruff call, this time far above him. He flashed his eyes upwards, searching angrily. At first he saw only sky, then he glimpsed it, plunging down over the poplars beyond Ivan's Meadow.

'Leave me alone!' he shouted. 'You . . . you bloody raven!'

He looked at the stone again, still sitting innocently in his hand.

'What is it about you? You're like . . . ' He tried to remember the story Mr Wilkins had read out in class about King Arthur. But it was no good: he'd never paid much attention to anything Mr Wilkins said, or any of the other teachers for that matter. He gazed desperately out over Mucky Meg.

This shouldn't be a problem. It should be easy. And

Mucky Meg was the perfect place: the one field with mud so deep he could guarantee no one would ever find the stone again.

One good throw and it's done, he told himself.

One good throw.

That's all.

In his mind he saw the stone fly over the field in a great arc and fall into the slush. Buried forever, in mist and mud.

But it was no use.

Holding it more tightly than ever, he turned, climbed the gate once more, and trudged back towards the house.

Benjamin stared down at his undrunk tea.

'I'm so hot,' he said, wiping his face. 'So hot.'

Toby watched him across the kitchen table.

Hot, hot, hot, he thought. Stupid idiot. Even his tea's gone cold. And he's slept through the whole morning yet again.

Mum drew up a chair next to Benjamin but Toby doubted even she'd get any sense out of him. He noticed Dad and Gordon had stayed out with the animals; probably they'd decided it was best to leave the talking to Mum. Or maybe they were just fed up with the whole thing.

The chill now seeped through the whole house. But still no one had mentioned it.

Benjamin's eyes rolled round the room.

'It's like . . . breath,' he said. 'Hot breath.'

'Well, I'm cold,' said Toby.

Mum frowned at him and took one of Benjamin's hands.

'Benjamin, you don't have to tell us anything if you really don't want to. But you must understand, we've been worried about you. Wandering about on your own. Up at Dragon's Rock. In the dark.'

Benjamin stared vacantly ahead and his lips moved, the words just audible.

'I had to . . . try and find it.'

'Find what?' said Mum.

His eyes fixed on Toby.

'What I lost.'

The back door opened, and Dad and Gordon came in.

'Getting nippy out there,' said Dad. 'And the mist's up to the top of Mucky Meg.'

Gordon thrust his hands over the stove.

'How are you, Benjamin? Better?'

'He's hot,' said Toby.

'Maybe he's got a fever,' said Gordon.

'Do you want us to take you to the doctor?' said Mum.

Benjamin dreamily wiped his face again.

'I don't want to go to the doctor. I haven't got a fever. I just feel hot. Like there's a huge—'

'A huge what?' said Mum.

Toby watched the changing expressions on Benjamin's face and a recollection came from the day before: of the nightmare, and the sculpture lying on his bed.

'A huge dragon,' he said suddenly.

'Yes!' Benjamin's eyes were on him again. 'A huge dragon.'

'But where?' said Mum. 'Where do you see this dragon?'

'I don't see it, but I feel it. Here.' Benjamin spread his arms about him. 'Underneath us. We're standing on it.'

'Funny looking dragon,' said Toby. 'Looks more like a stone floor to me.'

'You lads better eat,' said Dad. 'It's half twelve.'

Mum stood up and reached for the frying pan.

'It's eggs or eggs. No grumbling, all right?'

'I'll help,' said Gordon.

She heated some fat, then cut some slices of bread and laid them under the grill. Gordon handed her the eggs, one at a time, and she broke them into the pan.

'Great team,' he said.

She chuckled and Toby could see Gordon's cheerfulness was doing some good.

'Fried bread, Toby?' she said.

'Yes, please.'

'Cut me a piece, will you? Benjamin?'

'Yes, please.'

'Cut a piece for Benjamin too.'

Toby took the bread knife, cut two large slices, and handed them to her. Out of the corner of his eye, he saw Benjamin walk over to the window where Dad was standing.

'What do you use Skinny Sam for?'

'Cattle. Not right now, of course. They're all inside.'

'Have you got lots?'

Dad grunted.

'Not any more. That's why we're giving sheep a try. Not that they're doing any better. Specially now we've got to get another dog.'

'But why haven't you got so many cattle any more?'

'Don't get me going on that subject.'

Gordon called over his shoulder from the stove.

'Disease, Benjamin. We used to have loads of cattle but things have got a bit tough lately.'

Lately? thought Toby. They've been tough for the last six years. And it started after Benjamin first came to stay.

'We've had disease several years running,' said Dad. 'Just about finished us. We're still trying to rebuild the herd.'

Mum walked over to the table with the first of the eggs.

'So no Christmas presents for anyone this year. Boys, get started, as you're going into Totnes.'

Gordon sat down at the table.

'Another year without Christmas presents. Well, at least we're used to it.' He caught Benjamin's eye and winked. 'She's only joking. By the way, Toby, funny looking bit of whittling in your room. What's it meant to be?'

Toby took his knife and fork with elaborate unconcern.

'Nothing special,' he said. 'Just a dragon.'

10

Gordon swung the Land Rover into an empty space in the top car park at Totnes and switched off the engine.

'OK, I've got several things to get. You two can—'

'Why's it called Dragon's Rock?' said Benjamin suddenly.

Gordon looked him over tolerantly and didn't seem taken aback by the abruptness of the question, or the fact that it was the first thing Benjamin had said since breakfast.

'Don't know. Don't think anyone does. I remember a load of people talking about it in the pub once. None of them knew either.'

'Somebody must know.'

'Maybe. They're not that bothered round our way. Everybody keeps clear of the place, case they bump into you-know-who. Nobody I know goes there.'

'Except Benjamin,' said Toby. 'And sheep.'

'Sheep?' said Benjamin.

Gordon nodded.

'Funny thing. If any of the sheep go missing, we generally find 'em round Dragon's Rock. Don't know why. But that's why we're so careful about fencing.'

Benjamin thought of the haunting mystery of the place; its beauty, its danger.

'What did the ruin use to be?'

'Don't really know. Farmhouse probably. It's been a ruin for donkey's years.'

'Who lived there?'

'No idea. Before my time. But they reckon the locals drove 'em out.'

'What for?'

Gordon opened the door and jumped out.

'Witchcraft,' he said and strode over to the ticket machine.

Toby saw Benjamin look his way and quickly jumped out, too, before the next question came. Luckily Gordon was soon back.

'Right, you two, I've got loads of places to go. Meet back here at half five. And don't—'

But again Benjamin interrupted him.

'Does the Wild Woman live at Dragon's Rock?'

And again, Gordon seemed unruffled.

'Nobody knows. She's been seen in lots of places. There are loads of stories about her. They say she eats beetles, slugs, birds, rabbits—'

'Hedgehogs,' said Toby.

'Don't know about hedgehogs.'

'She does, they all say she does.'

Gordon shrugged.

'Maybe. Some of the locals leave food out for her so she won't put a spell on their farms. They reckon she's the one who's sent all the bad luck these last few years.'

'Have other people had bad luck, then?' said Benjamin.

'Oh, yeah, it's not just us. Everybody's had trouble.'

'She's behind it,' said Toby. 'Everybody knows she's behind it. She's a witch, she's evil, she's really evil. They reckon she can take the form of animals and birds.'

'Come off it,' said Gordon.

'She can. I know she can.'

He remembered the raven wheeling overhead; the cat on the post, watching him.

'I know she can,' he said.

And Benjamin thought of the woman he had seen in the night, the tall woman, swathed in power; and of Ione, her slave, caught in that power, caught in a cage of fear, in a web she could not break.

Suffering the pain of the world.

'Do you leave food out for the Wild Woman?' he said.

67

Gordon shook his head.

'Dad won't allow it. But we've seen her after dark, drinking from the outside tap.'

'And looking in the bins,' said Toby.

'That was a tramp.'

'It was her, it was definitely her.'

Gordon gave Toby's scarf a playful tug; then his face grew serious.

'I'll tell you one thing about Dragon's Rock. Some people say they've seen smoke coming out of the ground either side of it. Like a dragon's nostrils, someone said. So maybe there is a dragon there. Maybe it's got a lair underneath the rock.'

'You never told me about the smoke,' said Toby.

Gordon chuckled.

'See you later.'

Toby wandered down towards the Narrows, not bothering to look behind to see whether Benjamin had followed, and fighting the urge to sleep which, despite the coldness still clinging to him, was starting to grow worse.

Gordon had already clumped off.

All this talk about Dragon's Rock and the Wild Woman. Of course, Benjamin had started it, as usual, but the surprising thing was that even Gordon didn't seem to understand how evil she was.

He frowned.

Maybe Benjamin was in league with the Wild Woman and all these questions were just to fool them. After all, he kept running away to Dragon's Rock, and he was the one who brought the stone to the farm in the first place; and it was then that the horrible cold presence arrived.

He plodded on through the Narrows and down to the square. Totnes was packed, presumably with late Christmas shoppers, he thought, looking morosely at them. He'd never felt less like Christmas in his life, and right now he could have done with some peace and quiet, to think things through. As though to taunt him further, a busker nearby started to play 'Silent Night' on an accordion.

He stomped on down the hill.

Everyone knows the Wild Woman's evil, he thought. Everyone knows she can take any form she likes. She was inside that raven, inside that cat, I know it.

He stopped suddenly.

She's inside Benjamin. She must be. That would explain everything. Benjamin's in her power.

He turned suspiciously.

But Benjamin was nowhere to be seen.

Benjamin didn't know how he came to be outside the bookshop. He remembered Gordon leaving them at the car park and Toby walking on ahead, clearly not wanting company.

At least, not *his* company.

He remembered darkness falling as he meandered about the town, passing several bookshops and not noticing much about any of them; yet feeling led by a strange compulsion. Then he was staring through a window at rows of books, and the image of a face forming in the glass.

At first he thought it was someone's reflection, but when he checked to see, he found there was no one behind him. He turned back and saw the image still there. Slowly it defined itself.

Ione.

Her beautiful, unmistakable features. But almost at once it started to fade.

'No!'

He reached forward and clutched at the glass. A man shouted from inside the shop.

'Hoy! Stop that!'

He stepped back, still peering at the window, and to his surprise found that where the image had been, his eye had fallen on a book. He read the title aloud.

'*Dragons in Landscape and Legend*.'

He dashed inside. The shopkeeper looked him over mistrustfully.

'What's up with you, then? Messing about with the glass.'

'I'm sorry, I . . . ' He squeezed past the man to the display stand by the window. 'I didn't mean . . . I just . . . '

The shopkeeper muttered something but asked no further questions. Benjamin reached eagerly for the book and opened it.

But his heart sank at once.

There was no message here. This book was far too difficult. It was much thicker than it had looked from outside, the writing was small, the paragraphs were long, it was full of maps and diagrams, and it cost far more money than he had, even if he'd wanted to buy it.

But there was no point in buying it anyway.

It would take a lifetime to read, and even then he wouldn't understand it. It was a work of scholarship for experts.

Not for him.

But the image he had seen stayed in his mind. He stared down at the book, certain that there must be something here.

On an impulse he closed his eyes, slammed the book shut, opened it at random and placed his finger blindly down one of the pages; then he opened his eyes and read the passage his finger had chosen.

' . . . and special thanks to my wife Dorothy for all her help and encouragement during the writing of this book, for typing up the manuscript and . . . '

He closed the book impatiently and tried again, this time keeping his eyes shut for some time, even after his finger had found a place on a new page.

'Give me a message,' he murmured, and opened his eyes again.

Almost in disbelief he found his finger on the blank backing sheet of one of the maps.

He stared out of the window. Soon he would have to go back and meet the others but he knew he couldn't leave yet. Out of the corner of his eye he sensed the shopkeeper watching. He turned his back to him and looked at the book.

One last try. One last try.

He screwed his eyes tight and held the book firmly closed; then, holding his breath, he opened it, stabbed his finger onto the page, opened his eyes and read.

' . . . of the theory that currents of power known as dragon paths run through the land. These are said to be especially powerful at certain points such as old church sites, mounds or standing stones in remote hills or valleys. It is from these key points that the dragon power is thought to flow over the landscape.'

He looked up, trembling.

Standing stones. Remote valleys.

Dragon power.

He read on.

'It is believed by some that the ancients understood and manipulated the dragon power for their own purposes, and that this power can still be invoked by persons sensitive to it, especially where the current is strongest.'

Power that can still be invoked, especially where the current is strongest. Already there had been witchcraft on that spot, if what Gordon said was true; then all the bad luck the farms had been having.

He wondered about the little stone he had found and lost.

Nearly half-past five. The shop would be closing and he'd have to get back to the car park. But he knew he had to read a little more.

'Whether the power was and is invoked for positive or negative ends is difficult to say. Perhaps the answer is both. But it is interesting to note how the symbolism of the

71

dragon has changed over the centuries. Whereas formerly the dragon was a symbol of life, fertility and harmony, now it has largely become a symbol of evil.'

He thought of the Wild Woman up at Dragon's Rock. And Ione, caught in a cage, a halter round her neck. Being slowly destroyed.

He had to help her escape.

Somehow.

He heard a sharp knock on the window close by and saw Toby scowling at him from the other side. Over his shoulder he heard the carping voice of the shopkeeper again.

'What is it about my window?'

He turned and saw the man standing there, hands on hips.

'If it's not you hitting the damn thing, it's your friend!'

Benjamin looked once more at Toby's face, then closed the book and replaced it on the stand.

'He's not my friend,' he said.

'I don't like the look of this,' said Gordon.

Toby came to with a start, suddenly aware that he had been secretly watching Benjamin all the way home to the exclusion of all else.

'What's wrong?' he said.

'See for yourself.'

The road before them had disappeared in mist.

'How far are we from home?' said Toby.

Gordon looked round, eyebrows raised.

'You been asleep or something?'

Toby shrugged. 'Sort of.'

'We're just down from the entrance.' He stared into the gloom. 'Darkness and mist together. Great, just what we need.'

'The lights don't seem to be doing much good,' said Benjamin.

Gordon leaned closer to the windscreen.

'We'll have to take it really slow. If you see anything, shout. I'm not bothered about the hedge but I don't want to bash into the oak.'

They edged their way into the mist, Gordon craning forward, his hands tight round the steering-wheel. Toby strained his eyes to see some familiar shape to guide them, but all he saw was billowing clouds. He noticed Benjamin staring at the floor, lost in thought.

'You might try and help, Benjamin.'

No answer.

'You listening, Benjamin? I said you might try and help.'

Benjamin looked up suddenly.

'You'll be glad when I'm gone, won't you?' he said.

Gordon sounded the horn.

'Cut the bickering, you two and—Christ!' He swerved suddenly. Toby heard something graze the side of the Land Rover.

'What was that?'

'The oak. We've gone past the entrance. I'll have to reverse. Keep your eyes peeled.'

'OK.'

They started to back and Toby narrowed his eyes, searching for a sight of the entrance; he knew it could only be a few yards away. There was a sudden jolt and the Land Rover stopped. He looked at Gordon.

'What happened?'

'We just found the oak. Didn't you see it?'

'Sorry.'

'Don't worry, I didn't either. We'll try and get round it.'

Gordon wrestled with the gear lever for a moment before finding first gear again. The Land Rover rumbled ahead a few yards.

'Now then.' Gordon twisted the wheel. 'Sing out if you see anything. You too, Benjamin.'

'What? What did . . . ?' Benjamin blinked as though he had just woken from a deep sleep.

73

'Never mind.' Gordon gritted his teeth and slipped the Land Rover into reverse again. 'Eyes skinned, everybody.'

They crept backwards, more slowly than before.

'There's the oak!' shouted Toby.

'Take your word for it,' said Gordon. 'Can you see the entrance?'

'No.'

Gordon leaned over Benjamin and opened the side window.

'It's got to be about here. Let's try it.'

He pushed the lever into first gear and turned the wheel; the Land Rover bumped round to the left and met no resistance.

They were through.

Toby felt the motion steady as Gordon found the centre of the track. Any moment now they should reach the back end of the shrubbery. He looked for signs of the fence but the ground was starting to feel uneven and he began to suspect Gordon had lost the track.

There was another jolt, this time in front.

'Blast!' said Gordon.

Toby leaned forward.

'What've we hit?'

'Shrubbery fence probably. Hang on.'

He jumped out of the Land Rover and wandered round to the front. Toby noticed uneasily how quickly his brother vanished from view, but fortunately he reappeared almost at once.

'Yep,' he said, slamming the door. 'It was the shrubbery fence.'

'Bust?'

'Well and truly. Can't do anything about it now.'

He reversed back onto the track, then drove on towards the unseen house.

To Toby's disgust, Benjamin seemed to have no interest at all in what was happening and was simply staring at the floor, as though nothing mattered but his own inner world.

The urge to reach out and hit him became almost irresistible.

He grew more certain than ever that Benjamin was in the power of the Wild Woman.

'We should be round the house by now,' said Gordon. 'Ah, we're in the yard. I can hear the gravel. We've made it.' He braked and switched off the engine. 'Can anyone see the house?'

Toby took his eyes from Benjamin and peered through the window. It was hard to believe that mist could be so thick. He, too, had heard the reassuring sound of gravel under the wheels and knew that the house was only yards away.

But he saw no sign of it at all.

'Come on,' said Gordon. 'Mum'll be worrying. We can find the way now.'

He jumped out and hurried towards where the house lay. Toby looked scornfully at Benjamin.

'You going to just sit there, then?'

Their eyes met, and Toby found himself wondering who was really watching him behind that faraway stare.

'I'm going in,' he said and, without waiting for Benjamin to move, climbed over him, jumped onto the gravel and plunged towards the house. Even here, only yards from home, he felt a wave of insecurity at the density of the mist, and the way it seemed to swirl about him.

Yet again he thought of the raven and the cat; and Benjamin's eyes.

The wall felt pleasantly solid under his hands and a moment later he saw the kitchen light to his right, then the open door.

A light touch on his shoulder made him jump.

But it was only Benjamin.

He shrugged away, surprised and a little angry that he hadn't heard Benjamin following across the gravel, and made for the light of the doorway. Gordon appeared in the entrance and gazed out into the mist.

'We're over here!' Toby called.

Gordon waited until they had reached the door.

'It wasn't you I was looking for,' he said, and gazed out again.

'What's wrong?' said Toby.

Gordon frowned.

'There's nobody here.'

11

At nine o'clock Gordon picked up the big lamp and beckoned Toby towards the back door.

'You and Benjamin stay here. I don't want you wandering off in this mist. I'll go out and see if I can find anything. Might as well look in on the cattle first.'

'But you know they're not there. They'd have heard us shouting.'

'Maybe, but I'll have a look. Got to start somewhere. Anyway, like I said, you two stay put.'

Toby hesitated.

'Gordon?'

'Um?'

'Do you reckon the house is haunted?'

'What do you mean?'

Toby looked about him.

'It's so cold.'

He didn't say that the coldness had followed him to Totnes and back.

Gordon shrugged.

'What do you expect, a heat wave? It's Christmas Eve tomorrow, case you'd forgotten. I'm more bothered about Mum and Dad. They'd have left a note if they were planning on being out for any length of time.'

Toby nodded towards the stove where Benjamin sat, still lost in his thoughts, and lowered his voice.

'What are we going to do about him?'

'Not much we can do,' said Gordon, also in a low voice, 'but for God's sake, keep an eye on him. The last thing we want is him running off again.'

'He's getting worse,' said Toby. He saw Gordon raise his eyebrows and quickly added, 'And I'm not just saying that 'cause I don't like him.'

'Maybe. Anyway, don't let him out of your sight.' Gordon reached for the door. 'See you later.'

Toby watched him vanish in the mist and immediately wished he hadn't gone. He closed the door and turned to find Benjamin standing before him.

'Where's my stone?'

The voice was different: not whining or hesitant or shy. Almost bold.

'Where's my stone?'

He tried to look indifferent. 'Don't know what you mean.'

'You do. You took it. Where is it?'

Toby glared back, expecting Benjamin to drop his eyes, but to his surprise the gaze did not waver. He faked a yawn.

'I haven't got it.'

'Well, where have you hidden it?'

'Why all this fuss about a stone? There are hundreds of stones. I could easily find you a better one. And yours isn't that good anyway.'

'So you have got it!'

Toby silently cursed himself. But all was not lost; he hadn't actually admitted anything, and even if he did admit having the stone, he could still keep it. After all, it was only Benjamin's, and he could handle Benjamin.

'I haven't got your stupid stone,' he said. 'And even if I did have it, I don't see why I should give it to you. It doesn't belong to you.'

Without warning Benjamin jumped. Momentarily taken aback, Toby fell to the floor, Benjamin's squirming body on top of him.

'Give it back!' shouted Benjamin, raining punches down. 'Give it back!'

Toby twisted his head to avoid the fists but quickly

realized there was no danger. Benjamin was no fighter and there was no power behind the blows. He waited, choosing his moment, then rolled over, pinning Benjamin easily beneath him.

'You can't have your stone.'

'You have got it!'

'What if I have?'

He jumped up.

'You don't deserve to have it back. You've been nothing but trouble. Running off and making us all go and look for you. And all the stupid things you keep saying.'

Benjamin climbed slowly to his feet, eyes downcast, body shaking. Toby watched warily, waiting for another charge. Then Benjamin looked up.

Toby narrowed his eyes, determined not to be out-stared, determined to show in his gaze all the anger he felt. And he searched Benjamin's eyes for a similar rage.

But he saw no rage.

Only despair.

He gulped. He had not expected despair. He had expected anger, wanted anger even, to match his own and relieve his guilt. He stepped forward, unsure what he wanted to do.

'Benjamin, I—'

But Benjamin turned, threw open the door and raced out into the mist.

Toby ran to the threshold, Gordon's words of warning flooding ominously back. From somewhere in the yard he heard the sound of running feet.

Cautiously he edged down the steps and away from the house, which almost at once receded in the mist. The footsteps sounded further away now, but he could tell where they were heading.

He stumbled across the yard until his hands touched the paddock fence, felt along it to the end and plunged down the track towards Mucky Meg.

Cruk! Cruk! Cruk!

The raucous cry sounded overhead and he looked up; but saw only mist swirling. He fumbled on, straining to see something he knew.

Cruk! Cruk! Cruk!

Again he looked up, and again saw nothing but mist.

The sound of footsteps had ceased.

He felt the gate under his hand, climbed up and swung his leg over the top, and listened. At first he heard nothing, then, after a moment, the squelch of footsteps somewhere in Mucky Meg.

He jumped off the gate onto the muddy ground.

'Benjamin!'

The footsteps stopped.

'Benjamin! Come back!'

For a while there was silence; then a voice, nervous, suspicious.

'What do you want?'

'Where are you?'

'What do you want?'

'Come back to the farm.'

More silence; then the voice returned.

'What for?'

He tried to gauge the direction of the voice. It had come from somewhere to the right, or so he thought, but there was no sign of Benjamin. He tried again.

'There's no point in running away. We've got to stick together.'

Cruk! Cruk! Cruk!

The gruff call came again, high above him.

'Benjamin?'

'Leave me alone.'

'Come back.'

'What for? You don't want me here. Nobody wants me here.'

Toby thought of what Gordon would say if Benjamin wasn't back on his return and took a deep breath.

'We . . . do want you here,' he said, certain that Benjamin

would feel the lie as much as he did. Benjamin didn't speak; and that was sufficient answer.

He moved as quietly as he could towards where he had last heard the voice.

'So where are you going?' he called.

'What do you care?'

The voice had moved. More to the left.

He changed direction and crept closer, crouching low to the ground. He knew the answer to the next question but it was worth asking it just to get another bearing on the voice.

'Are you going to Dragon's Rock?'

'Maybe.'

Now it was dead ahead, and close. He stopped, anxious not to give himself away by the sound of his footsteps. He'd have to make sure his voice didn't sound too loud when he spoke again. Fortunately Benjamin spoke first, without prompting.

'You don't want me here. And you won't give me back my stone.'

There was the figure, blurred but recognizable. But Benjamin saw him at the same time.

'Leave me alone!' he shouted and bolted into the mist.

'Benjamin! Wait!'

He started forward but the mist folded round him like a cloak. He heard the spatter of mud as Benjamin sped away.

'Benjamin! Benjamin!'

He began to run after him.

But another sound had come. A new, frightening sound, this time above him. He looked up, his neck prickling.

The next moment the raven burst upon him.

12

Benjamin could not run for long.

The hotness he had felt for so long still hung about him, as did the breathing presence in the land. He remembered what the book had said about dragon power flowing over the landscape; and in the boggy ground of Mucky Meg, surrounded by mist, he began to feel a sense of smallness, as though he were but a parasite on the body of a huge, quivering monster.

Toby's shouts had stopped with a strange abruptness. He listened to be sure there were no footsteps in pursuit, then tried to think which way to go.

He had to keep his wits about him, he knew that. No mad running or all would be lost. He peered round at the clouds of mist: here and there they receded and he could see slushy ground stretching away for a few yards, but such patches were rare; he knew there would be little or no warning if he met anything.

Or anyone.

He stared into the mist, searching in vain for encouraging shapes.

The heat grew more oppressive and he stepped forward. It felt better to be moving, even with the tingling under his feet, and so far he was fairly sure of his direction.

He hadn't come to a fence so he must still be in Mucky Meg, and he was certain he'd run westward after leaving Toby. So that way he should either come to the sitka plantation or, if he'd strayed too far south, to the top of Skinny Sam.

Yet again he thought of Ione. Somehow he had to help

her escape from the Wild Woman. And if the Wild Woman came—

He clenched his fists and pushed forward. The heat was growing more intense, more stifling; he tried to inhale more slowly but the air seemed to choke him. He tripped and rolled onto his side in the mud.

'Idiot,' he said. 'Concentrate.'

He scrambled to his feet, his trousers now sodden and clinging to his legs, and struggled on. The ground started to feel firmer and he wondered if the fence were near. But no fence appeared. He stopped and listened.

All around him was a deep rumbling sound. He knelt down and put his head to the ground. And now he heard it more clearly: an endless, oceanic roar, like the respiration of a huge beast stirring.

He walked on, yearning for a glimpse of the fence, and his foot brushed against something hard. He bent down and felt his hand touch a tiny mound with some kind of root on top, or maybe a young tree. He walked on and found another, then another.

This didn't make sense. He hadn't come to a fence so he must still be in Mucky Meg, but he had been walking for some time and should have reached the edge of the field by now. Or perhaps he'd crossed the fence without realizing it. Somehow the mist seemed to cloud memory as well as sight.

The roaring sound around him grew more powerful.

He carried on, praying that the fence would appear. It did not, but a gap opened in the mist, not wide but enough of a clearance to see a patch of grass. He hurried forward, trying not to run. He could make out bushes now, and a line of small trees he'd not seen before, young ones with protective fencing round them, not like the spiny sitka spruce above Skinny Sam. And there was the fence.

He breathed out with relief. Nothing looked familiar but at least he'd come to the edge of the field, whether it was Mucky Meg or not. He climbed over the fence and slipped between the rows of trees, wondering what they were, and where he was.

Behind him the fence vanished as the passage in the mist closed.

He forced himself on, the mist still billowing around him but slightly more patchy than it had been. To his right he glimpsed a small clump of nettles and further ahead what seemed to be a line of tall conifers. He stumbled towards them, following another slender passage in the mist.

They weren't conifers; he could see that now that he was drawing nearer. They were some other kind of tree, though he didn't know which. No doubt Toby would know.

He stopped again.

Toby.

It would have been nice to be friends with Toby. He looked back the way he had come, and for a moment wondered where Toby was.

Toby threw himself to the side.

Too late.

A stinging pain like a knife blade stabbed into his temple.

He fell back, crying out. Before he could recover, the black shape was at his face.

Fluttering, jabbing.

He gulped in breath, flailed his arms.

Cruk! Cruk! Cruk!

The raven's wings brushed his face, its beak darting like a shower of arrows. Pricks of pain stung his cheeks and brow.

He ducked his head, trying to keep his eyes from the bird's beak, and thrashed his arms round his head. The jabs started on his legs, stomach, arms.

He drew his knees up and pressed his face down. The fluttering seemed all around him now, as though ten birds or more were attacking him.

The jabs started on his head. He struck out and felt his

arm smack against the body of the bird. The fluttering moved back to his legs. He cuffed downwards with his palm and hit the bird again.

Cruk! Cruk!

The jabbing ceased suddenly. He crouched over into a ball and waited, quivering. A moment later he felt a wing brush his hair as the bird flew away.

He stayed hunched over, breathing hard, his body still shaking, his head throbbing where the beak had done its work. And he was frightened, really frightened; but at least the bird had gone. Slowly he raised his head.

Instantly the beak skewered into his cheek.

Pain shot through him again. Now the fluttering was louder, fiercer, the jabbing harder, deeper, and only round his eyes. He threw his head back and rolled it from side to side, but the wings still beat over him, the feet of the raven almost in his mouth. He swept his arm across his face and brushed the bird to the left.

In a flash it was back over his eyes.

He thrust his arm up and pushed the bird to the other side. It clung to the hand and pecked at the palm.

'Get off! Get off!'

He shook his arm but still the bird hung there.

'Get off!'

He drove his other arm down, forced the bird off and kicked up. The action threw him on his back but he felt one foot connect.

The black shape soared up and was gone.

He struggled to his feet and looked about him. The mist still closed in on all sides, faceless, formless, fearsomely chill. He was so cold now, so cold, so frightened. For some reason he found himself wondering where Benjamin was.

Cruk! Cruk! Cruk!

There it was again, the loathsome call croaking through the mist. He crouched, his arms across his face, ready for the attack.

But none came.

Keeping his arms raised, he turned and swept his eyes about him. And as always, saw nothing but mist.

Cruk! Cruk! Cruk!

The call was further away now and receding but he kept his arms across his face and continued to turn and scan the cold, vaporous wall. Still he saw only mist, but even that was better than the hideous bird. He ventured a step forward, his arms still high, karate-style. The ground felt fairly hard so he took another step, and another. His left foot sank into slush.

He pulled it out and it made a large slurp, and for the first time he felt some relief. There was always something reassuring about Mucky Meg. He thought of the times he had played here, giggling at the rude sounds he could make in the mud.

Cruk! Cruk! Cruk!

The sound was barely audible now and he decided he was probably safe; but still he kept his arms raised, as he tried to work out what to do.

It shouldn't be too difficult to get back to the farmhouse. All he had to do was walk until he reached some part of the hedge or fence and follow that until he came to the north gate. There was nothing he could do about Benjamin now. It would be more sensible to get back to the house, even if he did have to face the music.

Besides, Benjamin might have returned. He certainly wouldn't be able to find his way to Dragon's Rock in this mist, and Mum and Dad should be home by now. He lowered his arms and stepped forward.

And the beak drove into his face.

He whirled round, his arm out, but the bird was coming from below, aiming for his throat. He pulled his hand back.

But he was not quick enough.

The beak plunged into his neck like a dart. He staggered, thrashing wildly, and saw the bird close in on his face.

With a shout, he turned and stumbled into the mist.

He felt the bird light on his shoulder, the wings swish

round his ears, the beak stab at his eyes. He shook his head, cried out, but the stabbing went on, and on, and on. He tripped and fell to the ground, and curled up, sobbing, his face pressed into the mud as he waited for the fluttering presence to return.

To his surprise it did not. And to his inexpressible relief he heard a footstep in the mud nearby. Almost choking with joy he rolled over.

And saw the Wild Woman standing there.

13

Gordon groped through the mist, trying to follow the sprawling beam from the lamp. At least the cattle sheds should be easy enough to find, though it was hard to believe they could be so near to the house and yet remain hidden from view.

Not that he expected to find Mum and Dad there, but it was worth checking. He crunched over the gravel in the yard, the sound of his steps sharp against the eerie silence, and flashed the beam to where the first shed should be.

'Come on, you bugger. Where are you?'

A second later he walked into it.

'Damn!'

He stepped back, slightly shaken, and shone the lamp ahead. Dimly it picked up the contours of the shed wall. He walked slowly forward and put his hand against it; it was moist and cool, but somewhat comforting. He carefully felt his way along until he came to the entrance, then, still holding the wall, he stabbed the beam into the shed.

All well with the cattle but no sign of Mum and Dad. He fumbled along to the second shed, but they were not there either.

The sheep, then.

He felt his way back along the wall as far as the gate into Big Willy and flashed the beam over the ground beyond.

Boot tracks.

Two sets, one smaller than the other, heading into the field. So that was what had happened: they'd gone out to the sheep and got caught in the mist. He climbed over the gate and started to follow the prints.

Just as well the ground in Big Willy was good and soft, though nothing like as slushy as Mucky Meg; but at least the prints were clear to see. He bent low as he walked, scanning the ground under the focus of the beam. And as he walked, he began to guess where they were going.

And why.

He frowned. If only Dad hadn't been so stubborn and insisted on moving the sheep to Big Willy: the one field where the fencing still needed to be checked over after the gale. He cupped his hands round his mouth.

'Dad! Mum!'

He listened, straining for a response, but heard nothing: no answering call, no sound of sheep even; only a strange, soughless silence. He hurried on after the footsteps. It was more important to find Mum and Dad than the animals, and they must have gone to check the fence first. Certainly the prints seemed to be leading that way, unless the mist had distorted his sense of direction.

On and on they went, Dad's to the left and slightly in front of Mum's, as though he were striding ahead. Here was the fence now and, as expected, there was a break. It was easy to see where the sheep had forced their way through. He searched the ground with the lamp, looking for signs that Mum and Dad had turned back. They surely wouldn't continue; it would be much more sensible to wait for the mist to clear before trying to find the animals. Besides, heading in this direction was never a good idea, whatever the weather conditions.

But the footprints did continue. And just up to the right he spotted something new. Something disturbing.

A third set of footprints tracking the others towards Dragon's Rock.

Benjamin heard the voice and stood rigid.

'Help me!' it called. 'Help me!'

'Ione!' he shouted and rushed forward. 'Where are you?'

89

'Help me!'

He gaped at the bulging clouds all around him, smothering even the tenuous passage he had followed since the fence.

'Where are you?'

There was no answer.

He blundered on and saw the outline of another fence. And on the other side, the figure.

'Ione!'

He stumbled towards it, filled with wonder at how she could have seen him so clearly. But that didn't matter; he had found her and everything would be all right now. Everything would—

He stopped suddenly.

'Ione?'

But the figure was gone.

He slumped to the ground.

'You were here,' he groaned. 'I heard your voice. I saw you. I know you were here.'

He tried to picture her face and found he could only remember her eyes. He'd never seen such beautiful eyes. And he knew he wouldn't rest until he'd seen them again. He stood up.

'I'll help you,' he said. 'I'll help you. I'll kill anyone who tries to hurt you.'

He climbed over the fence.

'Even the Wild Woman,' he said, and walked on into the mist.

Toby knew she had come for him.

She had power. He felt it rippling about her like the chilling presence that surrounded him, in the house, in his room, and now here amid the darkness and the mist, a power that reached inside him and held him like a hand of ice. And he knew that this woman was the architect of that darkness and that mist, and of the deep despair swelling within him. He wanted to jump up and run but his body felt like a dead thing, a sack of bones and flesh no longer his but hers. He felt his mouth open to shout.

But no sound came.

She was moving closer now. He heard the squelch of her boots again in the slush, saw the grotesque body lean towards him. Then her face sharpened into focus.

He recoiled.

Not from the hideousness of it; he had seen that before, though from a distance. But only now was he close enough to see where the real terror came from.

Her eyes.

Suddenly he was on his feet.

Running.

Mist clung to him like a bag over his face. He heard his breath pounding against it.

The face emerged from the mist.

Dead ahead.

He blundered to the left, panting, his feet plunging deep in the mud.

It appeared again. Still ahead.

He turned and stumbled back the way he had come.

Again it took shape.

Always before him.

He staggered to a halt and stared, praying that the face was a trick, that it would fade into the gloom. Then the eyes moved, and beneath them, uncoiling like a serpent, the body thickened and closed upon him once more.

This time he did not run. He knew now it was useless. But he also knew that somehow he had to resist. He heard a growl deep in the woman's throat, saw the mouth twitch into an obscene leer, like the smile of a dog.

He ran at her, fists clenched.

'Leave me alone, you bloody witch!'

He threw out a punch. But it never connected.

A hand squeezed the breath from his throat and forced him back. He struggled but the grip only tightened. The other hand started to claw his body. Wriggling with revulsion he tried to squirm free. Then suddenly he understood.

The stone. She's come for the stone.

But there was no time to think. Both hands were round his throat now, holding him in a vice that wrung all resistance from him. Then her eyes bore into his.

And that was the worst of all.

More than the jabbing beak of her demon-bird, more than anything she could ever do to his body, this was the worst. He saw himself suddenly, as though through her, a helpless bundle of fears, trembling, yearning, begging her eyes to release him.

But they did not release him.

Instead they spoke, with a dark inner growl he instantly comprehended. One word. One question. For the one thing this woman wanted from him.

Where? The eyes said, Where?

And as they drove down into him like a torrent, searching his mind for the answer, he felt deep within him the frail bubble of his secret stir and strain upward towards her, longing to give itself to her so that he could be free. But even as it rose, floating on the current of her will, he felt another part of him awake, a part he did not know existed, a part that reached out and snatched the bubble back.

He prayed that the defiance had shown in his face.

Her eyes blazed on, driving deeper into him until he no longer knew whether she had torn the secret from him or not.

Then she threw him to the ground and was gone.

92

14

Gordon burst into the house.

'Toby! I've found out where they've gone. They've—'

The silence of the house fell over him. He stood still, listening.

'Toby? Benjamin?'

Damn them!

They must be outside, and he could imagine at least one likely reason: they'd had an argument, Toby would have spoken his mind and Benjamin would have run off. Simple as that. It was plausible enough.

He quickly checked the house to make sure it was empty, then tore a piece of paper from the pad by the phone, scribbled a note and propped it up in the middle of the table.

'Right,' he said, and threw open the back door.

Outside the mist seemed thicker than ever.

'Toby! Benjamin!'

Still nothing, and that was bad. They must be some distance from the house if they couldn't hear him. But the boys would have to wait. He still had to try and find Mum and Dad. He thought of the third set of footprints following theirs towards Dragon's Rock, and shuddered.

But at least he had some clues.

'Come on,' he said. 'Move yourself.'

He cautiously made his way through the mist towards where he had left the Land Rover. At least that hadn't moved. He ran his hand over the bonnet and along the door; it was cold but pleasantly familiar and welcoming. He climbed in.

The dashboard and instruments relaxed him further:

everything in its place, everything as it should be. He started the engine and switched on the headlamps, but all they showed was an eddy of mist. He flicked onto main beam. As expected, that was worse, and he dipped them again.

'Ah well. Have to guess the way.'

He looked over his shoulder to where the house lay, now gobbled up by the mist, and pushed the gear lever into reverse.

'Careful now. Slowly, slowly.'

He eased up the clutch pedal and the Land Rover moved backwards. 'Not too fast. Left hand down. Stop!'

He slumped back in the seat. This was going to be even harder than he'd imagined. For a moment he toyed with the idea of walking, but quickly dismissed it. He'd need the Land Rover if he found the others and besides, he knew he'd feel safer with its solid bulk around him, despite the problems of driving through the mist. He thought over the various routes to Dragon's Rock.

No use heading over the fields. He might find his way down to Skinny Sam but he'd never navigate the Land Rover through the trees beyond the sitka plantation. The track along the top of Mucky Meg could be worse. Even if he did dodge the trees, the ground was so treacherous and uneven he could only envisage a blind, frantic journey, the Land Rover bucking and barging through the hollows, maybe crashing and leaving him stranded in the murky environs of Dragon's Rock.

And there was no warning of the little valley; the trees ended and the ground fell straightaway. He shivered at the prospect.

The road, then.

Take it slow, one thing at a time. Swing the old bus into the centre of the track and stay there. Get past the house, left out of the farm and down the lane as far as the road. Left again and carry on till you reach the old track up to the ruin.

If it's still there, and if it's passable. It must be a long time since anyone used it.

It was hard to believe that the old ruin he had avoided since the day the family moved here had ever been lived in.

He peered about him.

With the mist as thick as this, the bends in the road near the Dragon's Rock entrance would be almost invisible. He stared along the beam. Two, three feet, it seemed, before it died away.

'Come on,' he said. 'Bite the bullet.'

He tried to gauge where the centre of the yard would be, pushed the lever into first gear and eased in the clutch. The Land Rover edged forward into the gloom and almost immediately bumped and reared. He braked sharply, opened the door and bent close to the ground.

He'd driven up the rockery.

This was hopeless; he hadn't even found his way out of the yard and he was off course.

Yet again he peered about him. But there was nothing to see: no house, no fence, no cattle sheds, no track. He slammed the door and started to reverse. Almost at once the Land Rover crunched into something.

He cursed and braked again. But at least he didn't need to look this time to see what he had hit. Too bad. The paddock fence would have to wait. He must have turned the wheel too far. He stared in front and tried to work out where to aim next.

Straight ahead. Give it about twenty yards, then right.

Slowly, slowly, he told himself, as the Land Rover slid forward again. He felt the left side of the vehicle lift. It had to be the rockery but he wasn't going to stop this time. He turned the wheel a fraction to the right and a moment later the Land Rover thumped down again.

So much for the rockery. He thought of the next obstacle to negotiate.

The side of the house.

'Keep left, keep left.'

Better to shave the outside of the cattle shed than crash into the house. The crackle of gravel under the wheels was gone and he knew he must be somewhere near the corner of the house. He slowed down, trying to guess when he would be past and free to turn right along the orchard.

The front of the Land Rover plunged into a spongy mass. Shoots spattered against the windscreen like tiny fists. He braked again.

'Think we've gone a bit too far.'

He pulled back from the hedge and swung the Land Rover round to the right.

'Hang on, not full lock. Stay close.'

Better to let the left side of the Land Rover brush the hedge on the way down the track; at least that way he should stay on course. The motion was bumpier but he expected that, being on the edge of the track, and trying to fumble down the centre would be more risky; he could easily skew off to the right and hit one of the apple trees.

He brought the Land Rover closer to the hedge until he could hear the scratching and scraping against the side, and see the branches ahead dancing in the beam before the Land Rover nosed them away. The mist was growing thicker as he quarried a path through it towards the end of the track. Before much longer he should come to the farm entrance. But the windscreen was moistening and every so often the Land Rover bounced away towards the centre of the track, making him jerk the wheel back.

He switched on the wipers, leaned forward and tried to follow the beam. But all he saw was a pale fan-shape where the hedge ran to the left, and that was fading. If he lost sight of the hedge, he would have to stop.

But he couldn't stop. He had to get to Dragon's Rock. Somehow.

To his relief, the mist fell back a few yards and he found he could see further along the track.

'About time too,' he muttered. The prospect of crawling at five miles an hour all the way to Dragon's Rock had been

96

lowering his spirits, but now it looked as though the mist was clearing after all. He thought of Mum and Dad again, changed gear and put on speed. There was no time to waste.

The shape came at him so quickly he remembered little: his own scream; a rushed recognition; a flash of guilt. That he had been over-confident, that he was going too fast; that the mist was still dangerous.

That he should have thought of the oak.

He heard the crash. But nothing more.

15

Benjamin pressed himself against the broken-down wall of the outhouse, shaking from exhaustion, and looked at his watch.

To his surprise he saw it was three in the morning.

How long, he wondered, had he been stumbling about in the mist. It was hard to believe that it had been so many hours. But at least he had reached the first outhouse. He remembered there had been three, each one crumbly and abandoned, when he came here all those years ago, so this time he must have come in from the east and avoided the little valley. He felt his way round the outside of the building.

Somewhere nearby Ione must be hiding; he could sense her and he was sure she must sense him. But she would be frightened. He knew she would be frightened.

Just as he was.

He looked about him, searching for the Wild Woman's face.

At least the mist hid him as it hid her, though he had the disconcerting feeling that she had created it and was not affected by it at all. He was feeling hotter and hotter, and the roaring sound was still with him, louder than ever. It did not feel evil, but it felt powerful; as though the land itself were yawning as it woke from an unsettled sleep.

He thought of the dragon again.

'Come on,' he said aloud. 'You can't stay here.'

He had to find Ione, had to rescue her. He might have lost the stone and made the dragon angry, as Ione had said, but he could still do some good. And he knew where he had to go: the one place his instinct told him not to go, but the one place that might hold the key.

He tried to push his fear aside.

'Don't chicken out now. For God's sake, don't chicken out now.'

He had to find the courage to look for her, despite the danger of being caught by the Wild Woman. If he could only find Ione first, alone, there was a chance. Not that he knew how he was going to persuade her to leave this place and come back with him to the world. Maybe she wouldn't come. Maybe she'd refuse.

Then he would stay. And they'd face the Wild Woman together.

He waited a moment longer, wiping the sweat from his face and listening to the unending roar; then he slipped away from the outhouse. Somewhere in this direction, if he remembered correctly, there should be another outhouse. He scurried forward, arms outstretched.

Please, he said silently, please let me—

He barged into something and stepped back, a little dazed. But he knew his prayer had been answered.

He'd reached the next outhouse.

He felt his way round it, struggling to catch a recognizable shape. Somewhere here, perhaps only inches away, he'd meet the person he sought. Or the one he dreaded.

He ran into the mist again, praying as before that he would come to the next outhouse. But this time he did not. He drew up quickly, glancing tensely about him. Perhaps he hadn't come in from the east after all, perhaps he was going the other way, back towards the farm; or perhaps he'd just missed the third outhouse. He took off his glasses, wiped them and put them back on.

Walk on, he decided, and stepped forward.

To his amazement, the mist fell away as though a curtain had been drawn back, and he found himself in a moonlit clearing.

Before him was the ruined house, standing stiff and gaunt like a sentinel over the valley from whose belly the rock rose, wrapped in mystery.

He looked back and saw the mist gliding like a moat.

Courage, he told himself. For Ione's sake.

This wasn't the time to give in. He had to try and save her before the Wild Woman destroyed her. It might be too late already.

But he tried not to think of that possibility.

He ran forward and pushed himself against the side of the house, glancing feverishly about him. Nothing stirred in the darkness.

Courage. For Ione's sake.

He looked along the wall of the ruin and memories flooded back, more now from the smell of the place than from what his eyes remembered. But then, he had not been inside when he was eight; he had come to Dragon's Rock from another direction, taken the stone and run up the slope and away, past this place, hurrying home with his prize.

And his guilt.

But now he was here again, touching its shell, smelling its decay, feeling its pain. And this time he would go in.

He crept along to the first glassless window and looked in. All was dark inside but gradually his eyes made out the shape of an old fireplace forlornly standing on the far side.

An empty room, nothing more. Perhaps a living-room once.

But a dead room now.

He heard an owl call and glanced over his shoulder.

Courage, courage. Don't run away.

He stole to the next window. Another empty room, also with a fireplace; perhaps a dining-room or kitchen once. He tiptoed round the back of the house but there were no windows on this side. He looked up and saw moonlight brightening what was left of the roof. And to his surprise he found himself wishing Toby were here.

Toby would have plenty of courage.

He crept round the house, peeping in all the windows but there was no sign that anybody had been here for a very long time. At last he came to the opening that had once held the front door.

From inside came an odour of damp and mould. He peered round and saw a dark hallway, the ceiling still intact, unlike some of the rooms where the roof had caved in above and left them exposed. At the end of the hall he saw the outline of a stairway.

Anybody living here would use one of the downstairs rooms where there was a ceiling for shelter, he decided. They wouldn't use the upstairs as there was hardly any roof. So there was no point in going up.

He gritted his teeth and walked towards the stairs.

His mind was racing with fear now. He tried to relax, tried to tell himself there was nothing to be afraid of upstairs, and that he was just going to look for clues. He braced himself and ran up.

But all was well: half of the upstairs was open to the sky and what roof remained was rotten; there was nobody up here. He turned to walk back down.

And tensed.

Down below was a large stone slab, part of the old flagstone floor. Innocent enough, it seemed, yet from where he stood, he could see as the moonlight caught it that it was not snug and square like the others.

Someone at some time had moved it.

He walked slowly down, telling himself that there was nothing to worry about, that whoever had moved it and not replaced it properly probably did so years ago and was long gone; that it was hardly worth bothering to check it over.

He bent down and, with an effort, pulled the slab to the side.

Underneath was a tunnel leading down below the house. Just big enough for a man.

Or a woman.

He stared at it and at the choice that now faced him: to run or to confront. Sweating with fear, he lowered himself down.

His feet soon touched the ground, and he sat down for a moment and peered up at the floor just above him; then, after a moment's thought, he reached up and pulled the slab back.

Darkness enveloped him at once.

He lowered his head and crawled forward, following a tunnel he could not see but which felt strangely hard and bony wherever he touched it. It was twisting downwards, that much was clear, away from the house, away from the air, and into a realm he could not foresee. He wondered who built this tunnel, who used it.

And where that person was.

Now he could see an eerie glimmer reaching up towards him, illuminating the sides of the tunnel so that it looked like a giant worm sliding down into the earth. And with that impression came another, stranger still: that the body of the worm had ribs. Then, as he looked more closely, he saw why.

The walls and ceiling were covered with a curious latticework, a crisscross ornamentation of sticks woven to a wattle skin. He stared at it, remembering the sticks he had seen Ione with that day, sticks just like these. But those had been for a cage, she said; a cage she was being forced to make.

He looked over his shoulder, wondering again who roamed this place.

The jailer or the slave?

The roaring had grown louder. He crawled on, closer and closer to the light, and the more he did so, the more the roar intensified. He stopped again, trying to discover the source of the sound. One moment it seemed all around him; the next, inside his head. He remembered a time in church when the choir had sung a long 'Amen' that seemed to go on for ever. This sounded like an 'Amen' too, and it really did go on for ever.

But he was not in church now.

And he was feeling hotter, hotter, hotter.

The tunnel dipped and came to an end. And to his amazement he found himself standing in a vast underground cave.

He stared round in wonder. The light came from a candle pushed in the earth and by its glow he saw boxes and crates and old plastic bags thrown together in a corner. What was in them he could not tell. In the middle of the cave was a small bed made from coarse bits of timber, roughly nailed together; no mattress or pillow or sheets, just hard boards and a large old blanket thrown over.

Stuck in the ground on the far side of the bed was a long knife.

He walked nervously past it and saw, beneath an overhang in the rock, the remains of a fire. Cautiously he bent over the cinders and looked up. Two slender shafts reached towards the ground above, clear, he presumed, or the fire wouldn't work. Then he remembered what Gordon had said about people seeing smoke coming from around the rock, thinking it was from the dragon's nostrils. But if the smoke came from here—

He wheeled round.

The cave must be directly beneath the rock.

He glanced about him, again wondering about this place. It could be Ione's cell. That was possible. He'd seen the sticks. But it could be the Wild Woman's lair. And Ione could be dead.

Then he saw the markings on the ceiling.

Deep, clear markings, scratched there, he knew, by the same hand that had gouged the tunnel, covering the roof of the cave with a huge fearsome shape.

The face of a dragon.

The roar seemed to split his head, the heat to smother him. He staggered back and kicked the knife so that it quivered in the ground. The next moment he was stumbling for the tunnel.

He had to get out. Back to the surface. Ione wasn't here and he had to help her, if she was still alive. And this was a terrifying place.

He scrambled up the tunnel as fast as he could, breathing harder and harder in his desperation to reach the top. But as he drew near, he heard a sound he had been dreading.

The sound of the slab moving above him.

16

Toby lost all track of time, all track of reality. As in a macabre dream, he floundered in the sea of his hatred, struggling to find relief.

There was none.

He was running, falling, running, falling, finding only mist and mud and madness, and longing for revenge. Then he was lying in the mud, his body shivering like the string of a hideous instrument, plucked and left to vibrate out of tune by some malicious, discarnate being.

Don't give in, he told himself.

Don't let her win.

He stood up and plunged into the mist, not knowing where he was going, aware only that he must move, must find his way back to the house. He felt dangerously cold and knew panic was still near.

Cruk! Cruk! Cruk!

He ducked at once, hands over his face.

No attack came; but he had thought that before. He pushed on, head lowered, shoulders hunched.

Keep walking, keep walking.

His feet made the familiar sucking sound as he pulled them out of the mud and he tried to think which part of Mucky Meg had slush as deep as this. But there were many parts of the field it could be. He stopped and looked around him.

This was stupid: he only had to keep walking straight until he came to the border of the field. If he was heading away from the gate along the top of the field, he should end up at the hedgerow on the west side, just below the forest;

and if he was going south, he would end up at Skinny Sam. Maybe he was already heading towards the gate.

He frowned. Or east. Or round in circles.

As if to taunt him, he saw bootprints in the mud, cutting off to the right. He placed his foot inside the nearest one.

A perfect fit.

'Damn!' he said. Then he spotted tractor marks nearby, trac-tracks as Gordon called them, running off into the mist. He bent over and studied them.

'Please take me to the gate. Please.'

At first they were easy enough to follow, then the mud hardened and he lost them for a few yards. He bent closer to the ground and spotted more trac-tracks further on, heading in the same direction, scrambled after them and a moment later saw the outline of the hedge to the right.

It was the north side of the field after all. He hurried along the hedge and almost at once came upon the gate. Looking cautiously about him, he climbed over and edged his way towards where the farmhouse lay, still hidden in the mist.

The paddock fence was not yet in view but he could just make out the dusky shape of the hedgerows on either side. The mist seemed to be clearing slightly but it was still dark and cold. He tried to think of what he would say. Gordon should be back by now, hopefully with Mum and Dad; maybe Benjamin too.

First of all, own up about the stone. If Benjamin's there, go and get it and give it back to him in front of everybody. Then tell them about the Wild Woman.

And if Benjamin's not there—

He stopped, frowning.

I'll just have to face the music.

But despite his good intentions, he felt hatred rising again. Hatred for Benjamin, for the Wild Woman, for the stone.

He caught the scent of newly-treated wood and the paddock fence appeared; he reached out and ran his hand down the overlapping timbers as he made his way towards the yard. The mist was definitely clearing, yet even here on familiar ground he sensed danger. He walked on, more slowly, and saw the silver birch before him and ahead, a speck of light.

The kitchen.

It couldn't be anything else, though the light was very faint. He left the fence, following the light now, and felt gravel under his feet. Then the house took form before him.

He was right: it was the kitchen, and the only room that seemed to have any light. He opened the back door and stepped in.

The moment he entered he knew something was wrong.

The light was on but cast no welcoming glow over the room, nor was the remnant warmth from the deserted stove sufficient to counter the creeping chill that had made itself his companion.

'Anybody here?' he shouted.

All was silent.

He walked to the hall door and opened it. Everywhere was dark. He switched on the light by the door; from inside the bulb came a faint whir, and a taper of light slid grudgingly out. He hesitated, then walked through to the living-room and switched on the lights there.

It too was cheerless and chill, the half-dressed Christmas tree no match for the air of dejection that permeated the house. No fire burned in the grate and all the radiators were cold.

He saw a face and jumped back.

Then relaxed.

It was his own, caught in the mirror.

'Clothes,' he muttered. 'Be practical. Clothes first, then light the fire.'

He wondered dully when he last slept and how long it would be before he could sleep again. If only he could curl up in bed right now and forget all this, and wake up tomorrow and find everything all right again.

But he knew there would be no sleep tonight.

He walked back to the foot of the stairs. Above him the landing seemed sombre and forbidding. Somehow he didn't want to go up, though he knew he would have to some time to fetch the stone. He pulled open the hall cupboard and dug through the jackets and coats. There was the battered anorak, an old friend of many escapades. Just as well he hadn't let Mum throw it away. He slipped it on, saw Gordon's old duffle coat and pulled that on too.

But he was still shivering.

He wished one of the others would come back, even Benjamin. Because although no one had answered him, he had a disquieting feeling that the house was not empty.

He walked back to the kitchen, usually such a happy place but now unwelcoming and cold, and his eye fell on the clock.

Four thirty! He stared at it. It couldn't possibly be four thirty. He'd only run out a short while ago.

Then he saw the note on the table.

A huge printed scrawl, clearly done in a great hurry but immediately recognizable as Gordon's.

TOBY/BENJAMIN
GONE TO DRAGON'S ROCK. DON'T FOLLOW. STAY AT HOME.
IF NOT BACK BY BREAKFAST, CALL POLICE.
GORDON.

He read the note twice.

Stay at home: the last thing he wanted to do, but it made sense. And there was something he had to collect; something he could no longer avoid.

He walked through to the foot of the stairs and looked up. The stillness of the house seemed to touch him like clammy skin and the landing looked dark and uninviting, the scant power from the lights somehow adding to the unseen menace he felt everywhere. He put a foot on the bottom step.

From upstairs came a scuffling sound.

17

When Gordon came to, all he saw was a blur. His head throbbed, his chest pounded; he felt pain in what seemed to be every part of his body. He tried to remember what had happened.

But memory was a blur too. A haze, a mist.

Mist.

The thought came more strongly.

Mist.

Something about mist.

'Mist . . . ' He heard a voice, his voice, mumbling the thought aloud. 'Mist . . . '

He sat up abruptly.

The pain in his head checked him at once. He clapped a hand to his brow and felt what could only be blood. Moving more cautiously, he stretched forward again, searching for something he knew, something that would tell him where he was. He felt a hard, sharp object under his fingers.

Glass.

A piece of glass, like a cube. A new image pushed its way into his mind, and with it came a third.

'Tree,' he said dreamily. 'There was a tree.'

His body sagged in the seat, aching for rest, but he forced himself to stay upright, despite the pain.

'Mist . . . glass . . . tree,' he said. 'Mist . . . glass . . . tree.'

The pain was growing worse.

'Mist-glass-tree. Mist-glass-tree.'

It was better saying it briskly, almost like the rhymes Mum used to teach them.

More images flooded in.

Mum. Rhymes.

'I had a . . . ' he started drowsily, 'I had a . . . little . . . a little . . . '

The throbbing in his head felt like hammer blows now, but he stumbled on through the rhyme.

' . . . a little nut tree. Nothing . . . would it bear.'

The words were coming, falteringly. He went on, moaning with the pain.

'But a silver nutmeg. And a . . . golden pear.'

This was stupid, chanting a nursery rhyme. He should be trying to work out where he was and what to do.

'The King of Spain's daughter,' he went on, but the rhyme was fading. 'The King of Spain's daughter . . . ' The blur over his eyes deepened, then inspiration came and he hurried on to the end.

'The King of Spain's daughter . . . came to visit me . . . and all for the sake of . . . my little nut tree.'

Tree.

The image was back and it was stronger than the others.

Nut tree. Birch tree. Oak tree.

Suddenly he remembered. And with remembrance came a chaos of pictures. Toby, Benjamin, Mum and Dad, tracks in the mud.

The accident.

He breathed slowly out; at least he was thinking again. But he knew he was badly hurt, and that if he moved too sharply, it could be serious. If only the concussion would clear so that he could see. He tried to focus his eyes but the blur was still there.

'Try moving your hands,' he said aloud.

That was all right, as long as he wasn't too vigorous. He lifted his left hand, held it close to his face and tried to read the digits on his watch.

That was no good; it looked like four something, which couldn't be right. He'd gone out around nine and couldn't possibly have been stuck here that long. But then, he was no longer sure of anything at the moment. He tried the watch again but this time the figures eluded him completely. His sight was getting worse and so was the pain.

He reached tentatively forward and traced round the shattered edge of the windscreen. Some of the glass seemed to be intact but there was a large gap where his head must have struck.

'Have to get that fixed,' he said. 'First job when I'm out of hospital.'

He stretched further forward and his chest touched the steering-wheel. Pain seared through him at once and he stiffened, groaning. It was easy to work out where the injuries had come from. Just as well he hadn't been going fast; but there'd be yet another lecture from Dad on seat belts. He ran his hand round until he found the ignition.

'Now then, battery,' he said. 'Let's see what you're made of.'

Somehow the engine struggled into life. He tried the headlamps, without success.

'Ah well. Can't see anyway.'

He thought of the others and tried the horn, but that, too, had ceased to work.

'Too bad,' he said. 'Just have to shout at pedestrians.'

He wondered why he was being so flippant. Perhaps because he could feel consciousness trying to leave him. Or because he was frightened it would never return.

This was doomed to failure, he told himself. If he had any brains, he'd sit here and wait for someone to find him. But he thrust that train of thought aside. He knew he had to get back to the house to call for an ambulance, and maybe the police, if the others still weren't back.

He pushed the gear lever into reverse.

'If we swing round on full lock, we should be facing the house.'

At least there should be room round the farm entrance to turn without hitting anything behind him, as long as he didn't go back too far. He edged the Land Rover backwards, the wheel hard down, and felt the vehicle cross the centre of the track.

'Easy, easy. Now straighten up.'

He found first gear and slowly let up the clutch pedal.

'Left a bit, we're bumping. We're off line.'

He adjusted the steering-wheel. That was better; the Land Rover was running more evenly. He tried to think of how he was going to find his way past the house.

'Safer to get out and walk,' he said. But he knew his body could not walk. Indeed, it was weakening by the second.

'Keep it slow,' he said. 'Really slow. Stop if you don't feel right.'

The Land Rover juddered on towards the farm and he leaned forward, straining to see some familiar outline. And as he did so, he felt the first flecks of snow upon his face.

18

Benjamin held his breath.

He knew he had heard the slab move but now, no matter how hard he listened, all he heard was the deep roar, resounding in the tunnel. Then another sound came, just above him, round the corner.

Someone scrambling towards him.

He stared into the darkness, uncertain what to do. It could be Ione. There was just a chance. But perhaps—

He looked frantically about him. But he knew there was only one place to hide.

As quickly and quietly as he could, he crawled back down to the cave, ran over to the bed and eased himself under, the blanket brushing his face as he did so. He felt dust in his nostrils and a pebble hard against his cheek. But before he could move it, he sensed someone standing behind him.

He waited, shaking, his legs drawn up to his chest, his heartbeat so loud he felt sure she must hear it. He was certain now that it was the Wild Woman, though she was still hidden from view. Holding himself rigid, he stared towards the base of the opposite wall, at the knife stuck in the ground.

She had stopped, somewhere behind him.

He was going to scream. He knew it. Any moment now he was going to scream and give himself away. But he dare not scream. He dare not move or even breathe.

Somehow he felt she knew he was here. Perhaps she had already bent down at the other side of the bed; perhaps even at this moment she was looking at him.

Don't turn round.

Stay still.

Don't scream.

The urge to turn his head grew stronger. She must have heard his breathing by now, must have bent down, must be watching him. Any moment a hand would seize him from behind.

He heard her move round the foot of the bed towards the knife and stop again, but still he could not see her feet. Again he held his breath, his eyes fixed on the bright blade of the knife. Suddenly there was a new danger.

Sneezing.

Dust always made him sneeze. And already he could feel—

He opened his mouth and tried not to breathe through his nose; and, to his relief, the tickle in his nostrils went.

She moved again and for the first time he sensed in the corner of his eye the vague outline of her feet. In a moment she would bend down and see him.

She must know I'm here. She must. She'll have seen the slab's been moved. She's probably seen me under the bed.

She'll kill me.

A hand reached down and grasped the knife. But the face did not appear below the edge of the bed. And she straightened up again. He tried to imagine what she was doing: fingering the blade maybe, thinking of him, caught here, in her power.

Suddenly she turned and he heard her striding back towards the tunnel.

And she was gone.

He waited a few seconds, then quickly crawled out from under the bed. There was no time to waste. He knew what he had to do, no matter how dangerous it was. She had a knife and it might be for Ione. Somehow he had to follow her.

Without getting caught.

He crept up the tunnel, peering ahead to make sure she wasn't waiting for him. But she hadn't stopped. He heard the slab moved aside and replaced, crawled forward, waited a short while, then forced it aside and wriggled out, praying she wouldn't be standing over him.

She was not.

Through the doorway of the ruin he caught a glimpse of her back as she vanished into the nearest outhouse; the one he hadn't found on the way out because of the mist.

Mist!

He looked about him. The mist was gone. And it was snowing.

But the night could still shield him.

He slipped through the door and ran for the cover of the nearest tree. To his right, below the sharp cut of the brow, he saw Dragon's Rock, bright and mysterious, down in the base of the valley. He reached the tree and threw himself against it, then, keeping low, stole across the clearing towards the outhouse.

Like the ruin, it had no door, and there was no light to be seen through the opening. But he heard a voice: a man's voice, angry, confused.

'I've told you, we don't know anything about this bloody stone.'

Toby's father! He gasped. The tone was unmistakable. He crept forward, wondering what it meant, and whether Toby's mother could be in there too. At that moment he heard her speak.

'We're not hiding anything from you. I promise we're not.' The voice was softer, calmer, but there was fear in it. 'If we knew where it was, we'd tell you. You must untie us.'

He stiffened.

They were tied up. And the Wild Woman had a knife. He inched closer as Toby's father spoke again.

'Look, for God's sake, killing us won't do any good. We can't help you. We don't know anything about—' The voice rose suddenly. 'Don't touch her!'

From inside came a scream.

115

19

Toby looked warily up the stairs, listening again for the scuffling sound. But all was still.

Slowly, stealthily, he began to climb.

Never in his life had he felt so frightened. Each step seemed louder than the last, as though the boards themselves wanted to creak and betray him. Upstairs an ominous silence had fallen, as though whatever stalked the rooms had heard his approach and was waiting in readiness, perhaps watching him even now from some hidden corner as he ascended the stairs.

He reached the top, switched on the light and peered along the landing, then back down the banisters to what seemed the relative safety of the hall.

And the silence seemed to deepen.

For a while he stood there, stroking the banister rail where it curved round the top of the stairs and stretched along the landing towards his room. The wood was cool and shiny. He squeezed it hard and tried to stop the shaking in his hand, but it was no use; he could no more stop it moving than stop his stomach churning or the hairs on his neck rising. Yet he squeezed the wood even so, until his hand hurt.

There had been no further sounds.

He listened and listened, almost wanting to hear something, but the house was like a tomb. Running his hand along the banister rail, he tiptoed towards his room. The door was half-open but he could see the foot of the bed and his school bag on the floor. He stopped outside and listened again.

If the thing was inside his room, it would have heard him and be waiting there in the darkness; unless it had crept out and was behind him. He looked quickly over his shoulder.

But there was no sign of danger.

He stared back through the gap into his room, then pushed the door fully back. It swung inwards with a soft brush of the carpet and he surveyed the familiar shapes: bed, chair, dartboard, the desk he pretended to do his homework on.

All seemed reassuringly normal.

The next moment claws ripped into his hand.

He cried out in pain, whirled round and hit his elbow on the edge of the door. The claws released him and he took a step back, darting his eyes about the room.

But nowhere could he see the creature that had attacked him. He raised the hand to his lips; it was bleeding, throbbing, trembling more than ever. He shook it hard, feverishly scanning the room.

Somewhere in here the creature was lurking, watching him for certain, waiting to pounce again. He took another step back, still facing the room. Behind him he felt the edge of the door and cowered against it, glad that at least his back was protected.

Then he saw the eyes, coldly watching him from the corner.

He stared back, remembering the Wild Woman's eyes, and the body of the creature took shape.

It was the cat he had seen on the post.

Suddenly it jumped. He braced himself, but it had not sprung at him; it had bounded onto the bed and was scratching at the pillow with its claws.

He knew now what the cat wanted. And he knew how much he hated this animal, hated its unnatural presence in the house, the way it had attacked him, the way it was coolly picking its way through his room.

It had come from her. Like the raven. Like all evil things. Like Benjamin.

117

The pillow rolled back and the cat bent to sniff what it had come for.

Toby jumped.

The cat looked up and he caught a flash of its eyes; but only for a second. The next moment he had grasped it by the neck and twisted it on its side. The claws whipped round at once and he felt them tear into his hand. He squeezed the neck tight and threw the animal to the ground.

It lay still, momentarily stunned. Without hesitation he stamped on its head.

Trembling, he stood back from the corpse. His hand was still hurting but at least he knew what had made the noise. And now it was dead. That was one thing the Wild Woman wouldn't get back.

He picked up the stone and it felt warm and comforting. And to his surprise he saw it was glowing. He let it roll from side to side over his palm. And still it glowed, like a crystal.

'What are you?' he said.

He'd thought the stone was an evil thing, part of the malignant power in the house.

'Maybe you are evil,' he said, answering his thought. 'Maybe you're just pretending to be nice and friendly.'

He closed his hand round it and glared down at the corpse. 'Well, you're dead anyway.'

He heard an eerie cry behind him and spun round.

And saw two more eyes watching him from the doorway.

This cat did not wait but bounded straight at his face.

He raised an arm to protect himself. Claws tore his hand again, the same spot as before. He shouted and hit out. The cat slipped over his shoulder but clung to him somehow. He struck out again. It fell to the ground and darted under the bed.

Before he could move, it shot out again and sank its teeth into his shin. He kicked out and tried to shake it off. It clung on, biting, scratching, squealing. He kicked again but still it clung to the shin, and the pain was starting to tell. He kicked harder, over-balanced himself and fell back against the door, slamming it shut.

Madness and terror swept through his brain. He kicked harder, more frantically, but still the cat held on and the biting and scratching grew worse. He reached down to try and prise the animal away. The claws and teeth drove his hand back at once.

Suddenly the answer came.

Instantly he turned and kicked the wall, using the animal's body to cushion the blow. The cat yelped and Toby felt the first moment of satisfaction. He kicked again; it held on as tightly as ever but he could feel he had hurt it. He drew his foot back and kicked the wall again as hard as he could.

The cat stopped biting and scratching but somehow clung on still.

'Stay there, then,' he snarled, and kicked the wall again.

This time there was a loud squeal, and the body of the cat slithered onto the floor.

He knew he had killed it. But without a second thought he stamped on its head.

Shaking more than ever, he leaned against the wall. The wounds from the raven and the cats now smarted viciously. At his feet lay the two cats, so alike it was hard to remember which one he had killed first. He wondered how they had found their way into the house.

With something of a shock, he realized he was still holding the stone.

The new cry froze him to the spot. High, hateful, unearthly, this time outside the room. He squeezed the stone tight and listened.

It came again, this time longer, higher, louder. As though summoning other forces.

And summoning him.

He faced the enemy hidden behind the door.

119

'But I've got what you want.'

He pushed the stone into his pocket.

'And you won't get it or me without a fight.'

He opened the door a fraction and peeped out.

A gallery of eyes met him.

He shuddered and tried to move back, but the pressure of the eyes seemed to stab him into stillness. Cats covered the stairs, their black bodies undulating like sinewy, silken waves, their eyes glaring unwinkingly at him as one.

And he knew it was one eye that watched him. A single eye, from a single enemy. An enemy with many bodies.

He watched, mesmerized by the subtly moving darkness of the stairway and the soundless approach of the cats. Somehow he had to think. He knew he couldn't stay here. He had to escape and find the others. The window was much too high and there was nothing to climb down. If he'd had some rope or long enough sheets, it might have been possible. There was nothing else for it.

He would have to go down the stairs.

But the sight of the cats filled him with terror.

He tried to work out how many there were. Twenty, thirty, forty; hard to tell. It made no difference. Wherever he looked, he saw cats.

All with the same hunter's eyes.

He thought of the claws on his body, tearing, scratching, gouging; but he knew the cats had come for more than that. They moved closer, not hurrying, as though they knew they had him in their power. Many had reached the top of the stairs and were only feet from the door. Others followed, as far down the stairs as he could see before the banister rail cut them from view.

How many there might be downstairs he could only guess.

Closer and closer they came, the nearest animals low over the floor. He opened the door wider and flailed his arms.

'Go away!'

None of the cats stopped and the leader bared its teeth.

He shrank back, desperately trying to think of a means of escape. The landing now rolled with dark, slinking bodies. He shot a glance over the rail: the stairs too seemed to writhe and swell, some of the cats climbing on the backs of others on their way to the top. But for a moment it looked as though the base of the stairs might just be clear.

But jumping was out of the question. He'd sprain an ankle or break a leg for sure, and the cats would finish him off easily. Then, in a flash, the idea came. It was fraught with risk and if it failed, he knew he would be finished. He glanced quickly towards the rail, wishing he could have craned over to see whether more cats were coming through from the hall.

But he no longer dared take his eyes from the creatures that had come to destroy him.

It was time to act. For better or worse.

He took a step forward and made as if to kick the leading cat.

At the same moment, it jumped.

He saw, as though in slow motion, the coiled body uncurl into a shining shaft, claws outstretched and thrusting for his face. He saw his elbow rise to block, his right hand punch down.

The cat fell to the side.

At once it tensed for a second spring. Bodies across the landing twitched and flexed, ready to jump too.

With a wild shout he leapt astride the banister rail and pushed himself down.

Face-forward he torpedoed towards the ground.

In the mad rushing flight he saw cats jump up, squealing. He twisted his face from them and clung on. The hall loomed towards him.

Clear of cats.

The ground punched into him and he found himself rolling across the floor. He scrambled to his feet, stumbled through to the kitchen and slammed the door behind him.

Claws started scratching on the other side.

He raced out into the yard. To his surprise the mist was gone, the sky was starting to lighten in the east, and it was snowing hard.

By the silver birch he saw the Land Rover, parked askew, and a small figure peering through the window.

'Benjamin!' he bellowed.

Benjamin looked round and beckoned frantically.

'Toby! Toby! Quick!'

Toby ran across and saw Gordon's body slumped across the passenger seat.

'What's happened?'

'I don't know about Gordon. He's not dead, he's still breathing. But . . . but . . . it's the Wild Woman.'

Benjamin was gasping for air.

'She's got your mum and dad. She's got a knife. She—'

Toby grabbed him.

'Where are they?'

'Dragon's Rock. One of the outhouses. Tied up. The Wild Woman. She thinks . . . she thinks—'

Toby shook him.

'What? Speak, for God's sake!'

'She thinks they know where the stone is. I heard your mum scream. The Wild Woman . . . she might have . . . ' His voice trailed away.

Toby stared at him, a feeling of unreality unfolding in his mind and adding to the madness already there. It couldn't be true. Mum and Dad couldn't be dead. They couldn't possibly be. They'd be back soon. Any moment now probably.

And Gordon would wake up, and the cats and raven would go away, and everything would be all right again, and—

He lifted his face to the sky and shrieked.

'I'll get you, Wild Woman! I'll get you!'

He dug furiously into his pocket.

'Here's the bloody stone!' He clapped it into Benjamin's hand. 'Come on!'

'But what are you going to do?' said Benjamin.

Toby pulled open the driver's door.

'Kill her.'

20

'You sure you know how to do this?' said Benjamin.

'Shut up! See if you can help Gordon.'

Toby fumbled with the ignition key and managed to make the engine turn over. But it wouldn't fire.

'Try the choke,' said Benjamin.

'I was going to.' Toby looked helplessly about him.

'Over there.'

'I know that!'

'You pull it out.'

'I said shut up!'

He pulled the choke out and tried again. Still the engine wouldn't fire. Suddenly he stiffened.

In the wing mirror was the face of a cat.

Desperately he tried the engine again, and again.

'You'll flood it,' said Benjamin. 'Try half choke.'

'How come you know so much about it?'

He didn't listen for an answer. In the mirror he could see cats pouring into the yard behind them. He felt panic rising again, mingled with despair at the knowledge that all was lost, and that even if he did start the Land Rover, he wouldn't know how to drive it, despite his boasts to Benjamin.

Into the turmoil of his mind came a quiet voice.

'I'll drive if you like.'

'You?' He was about to scoff but something in Benjamin's face stopped him. 'You know how to drive?'

Benjamin nodded. Toby saw more cats in the mirror and hurriedly made up his mind.

'Move across. Quick.'

124

He eased himself over Gordon's unconscious body and made room for Benjamin.

Benjamin seated himself at the steering-wheel and reached for the ignition key.

'Maybe you didn't press the accelerator when you turned the key.'

'Can we just go?' snapped Toby. He saw more cats creeping into view in the wing mirror on the other side; Benjamin obviously hadn't spotted them yet, but he would as soon as he looked in the mirror. The engine burst into life.

'Sounds all right,' said Benjamin.

'Go on, then!' shouted Toby.

'Which way?'

'Straight ahead!'

The Land Rover rumbled forward. Toby looked in the wing mirror and saw cats surging after them, fanning out in a huge black arc, in contrast to the snowy surface of the ground.

Overhead he saw a dark shape, whirling.

He put a hand on Gordon's shoulder, wishing he knew what to do to help him. But at least his brother was still alive. He glanced at Benjamin and saw him leaning forward, his face set in concentration, hands tight round the wheel. Snow billowed in through the broken wind-screen.

'Which way?' said Benjamin. 'Down to Skinny Sam?'

'No, straight on.'

It was no use going through Mucky Meg. He'd have to get out to open the gate, the cats were still close, and they might get bogged down in the mud. The road was out of the question: they'd have to turn round and drive back towards the cats.

'We'll go through the forest,' he said.

'Will the Land Rover get through?'

Toby didn't know. He only knew that the ground would be treacherous and hard to see with the trees packed so closely together; and that there would be no warning of the valley below the ruin.

If they made it that far.

'We'll soon find out,' he muttered.

He checked overhead and saw the odious form, arrogantly spiralling, and behind them, the rolling black wake of cats; and wondered why Benjamin had said nothing about them. Perhaps he hadn't looked in the mirror or above him.

They plunged on down the track, past the gate and around the north-west tip of Mucky Meg. In another minute they would be among the trees.

He looked about him again.

The cats had fallen behind but the bird still wheeled above them, as though marking their position. He clenched his fists and leaned forward. Somewhere ahead was the Wild Woman. And a test he had to face. A test of strength and will.

He closed his eyes tight and thought, Kill, kill, kill.

Benjamin was watching the trees through the onrush of snow and knew they would have to choose a path soon. He looked at Toby for guidance and saw him with his eyes tightly shut.

Yet the anger flowed about him more than ever.

He thought miserably of Ione. Probably the Wild Woman had killed her, just like she'd killed Toby's parents. And he realized that he too had his anger.

'Toby,' he said. 'I want to kill the Wild Woman too.'

Toby opened his eyes, and they were glazed, hard, dangerous. Benjamin nodded ahead.

'Which way?'

'Keep to the right of that big tree. We'll come to the valley from the east. The forest's not so dense there.'

The track ended and all at once they were surrounded by trees. The ground became a tossing sea over which the Land Rover plunged and reared like a dinghy.

'Keep to the right!' shouted Toby.

They twisted past the big tree, Gordon's body bouncing with the vicious new motion.

'Which way now?' said Benjamin. 'We'll never get through that gap.'

'Left. See if you can cut back later.'

Benjamin wrestled with the steering-wheel.

'It's getting hard to steer.'

Toby said nothing. He was looking out of the window for cats. There was no sign of them, but he could still see the black speck above them as it broke into view through the gaps in the treetops.

'I'm cutting back now,' said Benjamin, turning the wheel without waiting for Toby to agree. He'd seen a gap to the right that looked familiar.

But he was wrong; he hadn't been here before. The gap ran a few yards, then opened into a small clearing. He braked to a halt.

'What are you stopping for?' said Toby.

Already he could see the bird dropping towards them.

'Trying to work out which way to go,' said Benjamin.

'Straight on! Quick! Don't stop here!'

Benjamin drove on into the trees, realizing it was best not to argue. Toby's face had darkened and his fists were pounding his thighs as he stared forward, searching the forest.

'There!' he shouted suddenly. 'Go past that tree. But be careful. We're close to the valley.'

The engine started to splutter.

'No!' said Benjamin. 'Don't die on me.'

'Look out!' shouted Toby.

The trees fell away. Round to the right were the outhouses and the ruin. Below them, the valley.

'Brake!' he yelled. 'Quick!'

Benjamin drove his foot at the pedal and missed. At the same moment, the bonnet rose and fell.

And hung there, swaying like a seesaw.

The Land Rover had mounted the verge at the top of the

valley and was stuck, the front wheels clear of the ground sloping down to the rock. The engine had stalled.

Toby glowered at him.

'You idiot! I need the Land Rover for what I've got to do.'

But Benjamin didn't hear him. He was gazing down in rapturous relief at the rock.

Ione was standing there looking up at him, her face as unforgettable and beautiful as ever, even from this distance. He sighed. So she was not dead after all.

Toby's voice cut in, fierce, determined.

'There she is. Let's get her.'

Benjamin whirled round. 'But that's my friend!'

'That's the Wild Woman. Come on. We'll have to manage without the Land Rover.'

'Wait a minute. You . . . you—'

But Toby wasn't listening.

'She used a knife. So can we. There's one in the bag behind you. Pass it to me.'

But Benjamin was scrambling for the door, the Land Rover rocking as his weight moved.

'Hey!' shouted Toby. 'What are you doing?'

Benjamin jumped out and raced down the slope towards the rock.

'Wait!' shouted Toby. 'Come—'

But there was no time to finish his words. The black shape screamed in from the sky through the gap in the windscreen. The next moment he was fighting for his life.

This time the anger of the bird was worse, the beak greedier for his eyes. He struck out, blindly, wildly. Still it fluttered round his face.

'Get off! Get off!'

He ducked his head. The stabbing started on his neck, ear, cheek. Somehow he forced the bird back through the windscreen. Shielding his eyes he looked out.

It waited, hovering over the bonnet. He raised his arm, ready for the next attack; then froze.

128

A cat had jumped onto the bonnet.

He looked out and the ground seemed to be moving all around him. There were cats everywhere, far more than he'd seen at the house, as though they could multiply at will. And this time he knew they would be quick. They had let him escape once; they would not do so again.

A second cat jumped onto the bonnet. The raven still hovered, a few feet above them, but they took no notice of it.

Only of him.

A score of cats waited, poised to spring onto the bonnet.

'Damn you, Wild Woman,' he murmured. 'Damn you.'

She'd done this. Killed his parents, ruined his life. He'd come to kill her and she was going to kill him. He thought of her down by the rock. Laughing at him, probably. As for Benjamin . . .

Stupid Benjamin. Thinking she's his friend. She'll probably kill him too.

Two more cats bounded onto the bonnet. And in that second, the plan formed. It was as mad and risky as the last one but there was no time to weigh the pros and cons. He knew he would have to act at once. Gritting his teeth, he edged himself towards the opening in the windscreen.

'Come on, then, kitties,' he said. 'Let's have a party.'

And slowly, slowly, he stretched forward towards them.

'So who are you?' said Benjamin. 'Tell me who you are?'

She stood by the rock, her face somehow more beautiful than ever amidst the falling snow.

'Who do you want me to be?'

'You can't be Ione *and* the Wild Woman. You can't be—'

'Both good and evil?' She ran her hand over the rock. 'We're all good and evil. What matters is which is stronger.'

He said nothing, no longer knowing what to believe. She watched him for a moment and seemed uncertain whether to speak further. Then she leaned forward.

129

'You must put the stone back. The things the ancients left us shouldn't be interfered with.'

He moved back from her.

'How do you know I've got it?'

She straightened up again and he relaxed slightly.

'I can sense it,' she said. 'Just like I sensed when it was coming back. I knew the farm had something to do with it. Then you told me how you took the stone and lost it. So I went dowsing for it. I felt sure I could find out where it was. Then yesterday I saw footprints leading to Dragon's Rock.'

Her eyes darkened.

'I thought it was more people coming to get me, so I followed, to keep track of where they were. But the mist came down, I got frightened and lost my way. Then I saw your friend in the field.'

Colour drained from her face.

'I could see he knew where the stone was. I could hear it calling for me from inside him. But he was full of hate. I tried to pluck up courage to ask him where it was, tell him to give it back, tell him it was no good to him. But he ran at me. It was all I could do to hold him off.'

She took a deep breath.

'I was terrified of him. He has so much hatred. It's like a coldness deep inside him. It spreads outwards, over everything, like the mist. It's worse with him than all the others.'

Despite himself, Benjamin took a step towards her again.

'What others?' he said.

She shivered.

'There've been lots. And now someone's found the tunnel to my cave. I dug it when they started hunting for me and it's kept me safe. But now I've seen footsteps inside. I can never hide there again.'

He looked at her, unsure what to tell her, what to ask her, what to do. Unsure of what she was.

'Why have you stayed here?' he said. 'Because of the rock?'

130

She shook her head.

'Because of the ruin.'

'The ruin?'

She looked up at it, the snow moistening her face.

'It was my family home. My ancestors found the stone in the rock and learnt its secret, but the locals mistrusted them, accused them of witchcraft and drove them out. Generations later my parents came back and tried to squat there, but they were driven out too. I was three years old.'

She shivered again. He studied her face, searching for the Wild Woman in the features. But the Wild Woman was not there. He remembered the figure he had seen standing by the rock, exactly where Ione now stood, and how it had terrified him. But the face had been obscured and it had been night-time; and perhaps his fears had done the rest.

But the knife and the scream: those things he hadn't imagined. He tried to keep his voice steady.

'Why did you kill Toby's parents?'

'Kill them?' She looked at him in surprise. 'I haven't killed them. I could never kill anyone. After I escaped from the boy in the field and found my way back to the ruin, I heard people approaching. I couldn't see them because the mist was still thick. But I remembered the footprints and thought they must be coming for me, like all the others.'

She wiped her face with her sleeve.

'They didn't talk and that made me suspicious, then they started looking round the outhouses. By that time I was sure they were after me. I picked up a stick to protect myself in case they saw me, then they came out. I panicked and hit them over the head. Knocked them both out.'

Images crowded into Benjamin's mind: of mist and darkness and unseen enemies; and a petrified woman. But still he did not know what to believe.

'I didn't mean to hurt them,' she said. 'I just wanted to knock them out and run away. Then I recognized them from the farm.'

She wiped her face again.

131

'I wanted to tell them I didn't kill their dog. And I thought they might know something about the stone. So before they came round, I tied them up. In case they hurt me.'

She paused to take in a quick breath.

'They didn't know anything about the stone. They said they'd come out looking for sheep. I went to untie them, then realized I'd thrown away the stick and didn't have any protection if they attacked me, so I went and got my knife. They thought I was going to kill them. When I bent down to cut the woman free, she screamed. She must have thought I was going to stab her.'

She shuddered.

'I cut the rope and ran off, and left her to untie him. They're probably back at the farm by now.'

Benjamin felt a sick premonition.

'Ione,' he said, 'Toby's come to kill you. It's my fault. He thinks you killed his mum and dad. I must tell him.'

'There's no point.' She looked at him wearily. 'What can you tell him?'

'That you haven't killed his mum and dad.'

'It makes no difference. His mind was made up long ago about me.'

'But he wants—'

'He wants to see the Wild Woman dead.' She stared at the ground, now bright with snow. 'And I do too.'

He moved closer, his hand on the stone in his pocket.

'But you're not the Wild Woman,' he said. 'You're Ione.'

'That's not what he sees. That's not what the world sees. I told you, I'm in a cage and the Wild Woman's my jailer. She's got a halter round my neck and she's destroying me. Why should I feel any love for her?'

He stared at the face he had only ever seen as beautiful.

'But I don't see the Wild Woman.'

'You're different. I told you that before.'

'But why do the others see the Wild Woman? Why does Toby?'

She turned to face the Land Rover at the top of the valley.

'When your mind's full of hate, you see demons everywhere.'

'Demons,' said Toby. 'That's what you are. Let's see what you can do.'

The cats on the bonnet hissed.

'Not enough of you,' he said. 'Not enough to get me.'

He watched the bodies slinking over the ground, brushing against the side of the Land Rover.

'Come on, little demons. Join your friends.'

As if in answer, three cats jumped up onto the bonnet.

'Still not enough to get me.'

The nearest cats moved closer, their eyes fixed upon him. The raven wheeled upwards but still circled the Land Rover. He looked anxiously over the side. If the cats on the bonnet jumped first, the plan wouldn't work.

Gordon moaned suddenly but did not open his eyes. Toby noticed snow on his brother's hair and shoulders where it had driven through the gap in the windscreen. It was strange to see Gordon helpless. He tried not to think of what the cats would do to him if they had the chance.

He leaned further over the bonnet towards the nearest cats. They crouched lower, watching malevolently.

'You can't handle me,' he said. 'Not on your own. You need help. Much more help. You need—'

Two more cats jumped onto the bonnet, then a third, a fourth, a fifth. The Land Rover tipped towards the front, but still wouldn't budge further.

'Not enough,' he said. 'We need more of you up here, loads more. Then we'll really have some fun. We'll—'

Before he could finish, the ground seemed to rise like a huge black wing as the rest of the cats jumped. The bonnet dipped under their weight and with a suddenness he had not expected, the Land Rover plunged down the slope.

* * *

133

'My time's come,' she said, looking quickly at him. 'It's up to you to look after the dragon now.'

Benjamin stared at her.

'But—'

'Put the stone back. You don't need it. Just put it back and the land'll have a chance.' She glanced up the slope again. 'And remember me.'

There was no time to answer. He had seen the Land Rover hurtling down.

She turned to face it, her back to the rock.

'You're the steward now,' she said.

The Land Rover thundered towards her. And suddenly he realized she was not going to move.

He ran forward, screaming.

'Ione! Get out of the way!'

21

Later, after the ambulance had left to take Gordon to hospital, they wandered down to the paddock fence. The snow had ceased to fall and the ground was smooth and soft but it was clear from the sky that there would be more showers later. The Land Rover stood by the silver birch, just as they had left it, both doors open, and much the worse for wear.

They hadn't spoken since the rock. But now Benjamin knew he had to ask.

'Why?' he said.

Toby didn't answer straightaway. He was watching his parents through the window of the kitchen and wondering at the bizarreness of everything: the house nice and warm again, Mum and Dad safely back, no cats or raven, no dead bodies in his room.

'Why what?' he said vaguely.

'Why did you swerve at the last minute?'

Toby traced a finger through the snow on top of the fence. This was odd too: talking to Benjamin. But for some reason it didn't seem so bad now.

He thought back to what he'd seen: the Land Rover charging down, cats jumping and sliding from the bonnet, the Wild Woman braced against the rock, gazing up at him as he gripped the wheel, yearning to kill.

'Something in her face,' he said. 'I don't know. She could have escaped, easily. Run to the side, behind the rock.' He frowned. 'But she didn't move. She just stood there. Then looked up at the sky, like she wanted to make it easy for me.'

He looked away.

'She was going to let me kill her. And I couldn't do it.'

Benjamin too thought back. But his picture was different. He remembered Ione, standing by the rock; the Land Rover swerving and rolling up the other slope; the snow blinding him as he ran.

And holding Toby, telling him it was all right.

Then turning, to find Ione gone.

Mum passed round the mugs of hot chocolate and switched on the Christmas tree lights.

'She didn't hurt us, Toby. Just this bump here where she knocked me out.'

Dad was stoking the fire.

'I've got one, too.' He touched a spot on his head and winced. 'I'll say one thing for that woman, she can pack a punch.'

'It wasn't a punch,' said Benjamin, before he could stop himself. 'She used a stick.'

They all looked round at him.

'How do you know?' said Toby.

Benjamin looked down, hoping they wouldn't question him further.

'Whatever it was,' said Dad, 'it damn well hurt. Still, we're all right now. I'm only sorry it's mucked up Christmas a bit. We'll have to see how Gordon is before we get going on presents and things.'

'But how did you get caught?' said Toby.

'Stupid really. Went out about half five and found the sheep had got out of Big Willy. Yes, yes, I know I should've listened to Gordon and checked the fence straight after the gale. Anyway, they got out and we set off to look for them. And down came the mist.'

'It was awful,' said Mum. 'I've never known a mist like it. We couldn't even see each other. We had to hold hands.'

'I didn't mind that bit,' said Dad.

Toby gave him an impatient glance.

136

'But what happened?'

'Got totally lost,' said Dad, 'that's what happened. Blundered about for hours, worrying about you lot wondering where we were, and whether you'd got back from Totnes OK. Couldn't see a thing. In the end we huddled under a tree and waited. Waste of time moving. Must have been midnight before it started to clear a bit.'

'Much later than that,' said Mum. 'I remember telling you it was nearly one and that was some time before we left the tree.'

'Maybe.' Dad took a sip of hot chocolate. 'Anyway, we wandered round again for ages and ages, and somehow or other ended up at one of the outhouses above Dragon's Rock. The mist was still too thick to get anywhere, so we went inside to see if it was clean enough to shelter in, but it was filthy. We came out and that was that. Crack on the head. When we came to, we found ourselves tied up.'

'But what did she want with you?' said Toby.

'It wasn't easy to understand her. She's got a funny way of talking. Some kind of a lisp and a really rough voice. And I'll tell you, she's even uglier close up.'

'And more frightening,' said Mum. 'I was really scared of her.'

Dad nodded.

'Anyway, she started going on about Flash. Something about him turning up at Dragon's Rock all the time and the only reason we kept seeing him with her was 'cause she was bringing him back to the farm, or so she claimed. Well, at least we know now where he used to go when he ran off. If it's true.'

'But why would he want to go up to Dragon's Rock?' said Toby.

'You know what a funny place it is, specially for sheep turning up there.'

'But there was something else,' said Mum. 'She said something about animals and birds being drawn to her.

137

About how Flash took a liking to her and kept trying to follow her.'

Benjamin remembered the robin hopping onto Ione's arm, and he held on to the image: so bright and clear in his mind, but so different from the picture the others were creating.

Dad sniffed. 'I didn't believe a word of that rubbish.'

'So was that all she wanted?' said Toby.

'She went on a bit about how she didn't kill Flash. Said she found him caught in the trap and was bending over to see if he was alive when Gordon appeared. She ran off but reckoned we maybe thought the trap belonged to her.'

'We did.'

'Well, she said it didn't, and it wasn't an animal trap but a man-trap someone had made to catch her. She reckoned she'd found lots of them over the years and said she'd buried them so they wouldn't be a danger to anyone else. I took all that stuff with a pinch of salt. Oh, and there was another thing. She seemed to think someone from our farm might have taken a stone of hers or something.'

Toby saw Mum's eyes rest on him for a moment. Dad threw a log on the fire.

'Lot of fuss about a bloody stone. Anyway, we told her we didn't know anything about it. Said we'd come out looking for sheep, and she let us go.'

'We still haven't found the sheep,' said Mum.

'I'll take another look after I've drunk this.' Dad's face grew stern. 'Now then, you two, I want to know what you were playing at taking the Land Rover out, specially with Gordon seriously hurt.'

Toby and Benjamin looked at each other.

'Well?' said Dad.

To Toby's surprise, Benjamin answered.

'It was my fault. I was up at Dragon's Rock. I heard you in the outhouse with Ione.'

'Who?' said Toby.

Benjamin looked at him.

'The Wild Woman.'

'What did you hear?' said Mum.

'I heard you scream. I thought she was going to kill you.'

'So did I. But she was only reaching down to cut the rope.'

'I ran back and got Toby. That's why we took the Land Rover. We wanted to try and save you.'

Save them? Toby thought. He remembered the despair, the anger, the sense of hopelessness; the feeling that they were already dead. And that his world had died with them.

It hadn't been about saving.

It had been about killing.

He wondered how much Benjamin would tell them; how much he himself would tell them.

'And who did the driving?' said Dad.

'I did,' said Benjamin.

'*You?*' Dad raised his eyebrows. 'Who taught you to drive?'

'Dad did. I kept pestering him to teach me and in the end he gave in. He used to take me out in the van and let me practise on some waste land.'

Dad drained his chocolate and looked from one to the other.

'Well, your motives were good enough, but I don't want you doing anything like that again. If you were worried, you should have called the police.' He reached for his pipe. 'Anyway, it doesn't look as though the Wild Woman'll be bothering us any more. Or anyone else for that matter.'

Benjamin sat up.

'What's happened to her?'

'She's gone, or so it appears. Been seen heading for the moor with a big pack on her back. I've just had a phone call from Brambles.'

'The next farm,' Mum explained to Benjamin. 'They're one of the farms that always leave food out for her.'

'She didn't touch it apparently,' said Dad. 'Went straight past and across the fields. In a hurry, they said. Didn't stop, didn't look back. Funny, I'd have thought she'd have taken the food if she had a journey in front of her.'

Benjamin thought back to that first meeting above the plantation: the wintry sky, the early morning stillness, Ione gathering sticks; refusing his assistance.

'She's got her pride,' he said.

The others were looking at him again. He turned away, not wanting to talk, and into his mind came another picture of her, a picture of her face as he had seen it in the window pane. And he wondered yet again what she really was.

A frightening woman or just a frightened one?

Good or evil? Or good and evil?

We're all good and evil, she'd said. What matters is which is stronger. And he thought, maybe it's only evil that sees evil, and good that sees good.

Toby's father stood up.

'Right,' he said, 'I've got things to do.'

But Toby stopped him.

'Have you and Mum been up to my room since you got back?'

''Course we have. First place we looked for you.'

'So you must have seen the . . . you know—'

'Seen the what?'

Toby saw only puzzlement on Dad's face; he looked over at Mum and found the same. And his own puzzlement deepened. He thought of the desperate fight, so fresh in his mind and so real: the claws, the teeth, the rippling bodies, the crunch of the skull under his foot. The weight of the animals on the bonnet.

'Cats,' he said. 'Everywhere. Over the landing, down the stairs. So many of them. I killed two. You must have—'

Mum and Dad looked more confused than ever. He turned frantically to Benjamin.

'You must have seen them! When we drove off, they were following. And up at the rock. You . . . you must have—'

140

Benjamin shook his head.

'The raven, then!' said Toby. 'Didn't you—?'

But he could see Benjamin knew nothing.

'More likely a crow,' said Dad. 'Don't get ravens round here. Up on the moor, round the coast. That's the place for ravens.'

'It was a raven! It attacked me. Look at my face.'

'Do I have to?'

'Dad!'

Dad studied him in mock seriousness.

'Ugly as ever. What's the problem?'

Toby angrily rolled up his trouser legs and held out his hands.

But there was not a single scratch mark.

Mum watched with unconcealed amusement.

'You don't seem to have come to too much harm. Whatever it was attacked you.'

Dad laughed.

'What with Benjamin's dragon and your cats—'

'And raven!'

'And raven, we're turning into a flipping zoo.' He looked at his watch. 'I'm off. I'll give the hospital a buzz in a couple of hours. See how Gordon's doing.'

Toby sat in silence for some time after Mum and Dad had left the room. Then he turned to Benjamin.

'Why doesn't anyone believe me?'

Benjamin looked at Toby's face and it seemed somehow different. He remembered something Ione had said about seeing demons everywhere when your mind's full of hate. But Toby didn't seem full of hate now. Perhaps there might even be a chance they could be friends one day. He hesitated.

'If you believe in my dragon, I'll believe in your demons.'

'Demons?'

Toby thought back.

Demons.

He had called them that, just before they jumped on the

141

bonnet and sent the Land Rover down the slope. Strange that Benjamin should use the word.

But lots of things were strange now.

He nodded slowly.

'I'll believe in your dragon.'

22

They set off together across the fields, walking in unaccustomed harmony. Neither spoke, yet for once there was no strain, no anger, no awkwardness. It had snowed again during lunch but obligingly stopped as they slipped quietly out of the house.

It hadn't seemed necessary for either of them to mention where they were going, even to each other. It had simply been understood between them.

To Benjamin, this was doubly strange. Firstly because he could never have foreseen any alliance with Toby, slender or otherwise, and secondly because he had always intended to take the stone back alone.

He knew he should have put it back earlier when he was with Ione. But things had happened so quickly: the Land Rover rushing down the slope, Toby trembling in the driver's seat, fighting tears, his foot pressed hard on the brake; Ione disappearing. The time had not been right.

But now it was right. And he was not alone after all.

They passed the gate at the top of Mucky Meg and wandered down the track, the snow already deep under their boots. He looked around him, trying to remember the features of the landscape he had known.

But he could not.

Everything was different now, as though the snow had altered not just the fields and hills but the whole vista of his life.

He looked at Toby, a few feet in front.

Certainly Toby was different.

And Toby felt different, though he didn't know why. He

had looked for the bird and the cats the moment he left the house. He had looked for the Wild Woman in dark places.

But he knew they had all gone; left his life forever. And the house was warm again. As for Benjamin . . .

He listened to the sound of Benjamin's boots in the snow behind him.

Benjamin was still a mystery.

But not an enemy. Not any more.

All the demons were gone now.

They stood at the top of the valley and looked down at the rock, rising solitary and proud from the snowy ground. Toby spoke for the first time.

'Is this where the dragon is?'

Benjamin spread his arms.

'It's everywhere, but this is where it's strongest.'

'How do you know?'

'I can hear its roar, feel its breath. That's why I've felt so hot all the time. Since I took the stone.'

He paused, unsure whether to risk derision, but for once Toby's face held no contempt. It was worth a gamble.

'The dragon was angry with me,' he said.

Surprisingly Toby didn't laugh, and when he spoke, his voice was unusually subdued.

'My demons are gone now. Do you think your dragon's gone too?'

Benjamin shook his head.

'My dragon will never go.'

They wandered down towards the rock, sliding in places where the snow made the slope more difficult. Half-way down Toby stopped and pointed up at the ruin.

'Look!'

Benjamin looked up eagerly, hoping for a second that it might be Ione.

But it was only sheep.

So they had come here after all.

144

Toby had already turned back to the rock.

'We'll deal with the sheep later. Dad'll have to get help from Brambles. They've got a couple of good dogs up there. Come on.'

They walked to the base of the valley and up to the rock. And to Benjamin it seemed to grow more immense, more awesome, more frightening than ever.

'What've we got to do, then?' said Toby.

Benjamin reached into his pocket and pulled out the stone.

'We've got to put this back.'

He held it tight for a moment, aware of the keenness of both their eyes upon it, then, not quite knowing why, he held it out.

'You do it.'

The confusion in Toby's face was almost comical, and he wondered somewhat mischievously whether it stemmed from shock at being offered the stone or anxiety at not knowing where it went.

Perhaps both.

Toby took the stone and studied it for a moment.

'I never thought of this but—' He held it up. 'Look, it's a miniature Dragon's Rock.'

Benjamin stared in amazement, wondering why he had never noticed the resemblance himself. But Toby was right. And the likeness was unnerving.

'So where does it go?' said Toby.

'I'll show you.'

He walked round the rock and tried to remember the spots where he had placed his feet.

'Have I got to climb it?' said Toby.

'It's a bit slippery. Maybe I should—'

'I can do it. Hold the stone while I go up.'

Toby cast his eye over the rock.

'No problem,' he said and expertly began to climb.

Benjamin watched, trying not to feel envious, and thinking back to his own climb all those years ago; a

145

climb he never should have made, a climb that had caused pain to others, and to the land.

And here was someone else putting it right. But perhaps there was some purpose in that.

He heard Toby call down.

'There's a little notch in the top. Is that where it goes?'

'Yes, but it must never come out again.'

Toby reached down.

'I won't take it out. Here, let's have it.'

Benjamin stared for the last time at the stone and suddenly it felt heavy in his hand, far beyond its normal weight; something too heavy to carry much longer.

'Take it,' he said. 'Quickly.'

Toby closed his hand round it and reached over the top of the rock. Benjamin turned away, unable to watch.

Toby jumped down again.

'But where's the dragon?' he said.

Benjamin looked up at the rock, then around the valley.

'It's here. In this place and all over the land.'

'And is it still angry with you?'

'No.'

'How do you know?'

'I don't feel hot any more. And . . . and the roar's not like it was. It's peaceful now, a sort of purring sound.'

Toby looked about him with a hint of his old impatience.

'Well, I can't see any dragon, or hear one. And I've been feeling cold.' He thought for a moment. 'Funny though, I don't feel cold now.' Then he chuckled. 'I reckon you're making it up about the dragon.'

'Like your demons? Your cats and raven?'

'They were real.'

Toby started to walk back up the slope.

'Come on, I'm knackered. I haven't slept the last two nights and we've got to tell Dad about the sheep. And it is Christmas Eve, remember.'

Christmas Eve!

Benjamin shook his head. He'd forgotten about

Christmas altogether. They took a few steps up the hill, then stopped for a last look at the rock.

'You did promise you'd believe in the dragon,' said Benjamin.

'I know,' said Toby. 'But I can't see it. You sure it's there?'

Benjamin nodded.

'It's there,' he said softly. 'I know it's there.'

And as he gazed towards the rock, it seemed to him suddenly that the snowy floor turned blue like a deep, still pool; and into that pool the rock fell, shattering the stillness and sending waves up and over him and away in all directions, as far as he could see. In that moment, unbearably fleeting, unutterably beautiful, he looked into the dragon's eye.

Toby saw only a rock.

And a valley.

And a small boy, crying.

'Come on, Benjamin,' he said.

Benjamin looked round, and the briefest of smiles passed between them. They set off back up the slope.

And Benjamin saw that the blue had melted into the white again, or maybe the white had melted into the blue; it didn't seem to matter which. All things would melt away in the end, he decided, like the snow now falling once again.

At least the dragon could rest in its lair and the land would have a chance, as Ione had wanted. He wondered what she meant about him being the steward.

'Benjamin! Come on!'

He'd fallen behind already. A few yards up the slope he saw Toby waiting for him. He stopped, breathing hard, expecting some impatient gibe. Toby bent down, scooped up some snow and with great deliberateness patted it into a snowball, looking Benjamin over playfully, as though choosing his spot. Then he flung his arm back and, with a great shout, hurled the snowball high over the valley.

Neither looked to see where it landed.

They had already turned for home.

Storm Catchers
ISBN 0 19 275200 6

Fin is devastated by guilt when his sister, Ella, is kidnapped. He should have been there to look after her, to save her from whoever snatched her from their isolated family home in the middle of a raging storm. And he should have looked after Sam, too, his little brother, not left him to go wandering on the cliff top, playing with an imaginary friend, and trying to 'catch the storm' as it blows out to sea.

As the kidnappers make their demands, Fin's guilt is replaced by a fierce determination to find his sister, by whatever means he can, and bring the criminals to justice. But as the drama unfolds, and long-held secrets are revealed, Fin begins to realize that Ella is not the only victim and that the real villain may be closer to home than he thought.

Shadows
ISBN 0 19 275159 X

Jamie's father keeps driving him on to win, to become a world squash champion. But Jamie can't take it any more and is desperate to get away.

Then he finds a girl hiding in his shed, and in helping her to escape from the danger that is pursuing her, he is at last able to deal with his own problems.

He realizes he can't run away for ever. He has to come out of the shadows and face up to his father, whatever the cost.

River Boy
Winner of the Carnegie Medal
ISBN 0 19 275158 1

Grandpa is dying. He can barely move his hands any more but, stubborn as ever, refuses to stay in hospital. He's determined to finish one last painting, 'River Boy' before he goes.

At first Jess can't understand his refusal to let go, but then she, too, becomes involved in the mysterious painting. And when she meets the river boy himself, she finds she is suddenly caught up in a challenge of her own that she must complete—before it's too late . . .

Midget
ISBN 0 19 275218 9

Midget doesn't have much going for him. He's fifteen years old, three foot tall, and puny as anything. He's trapped in a useless, twitching body he can't control, tortured by Seb, his cruel older brother, and can only communicate in grunts and gestures.

But Midget knows one thing—sailing. He dreams of sailing his own boat, and showing Seb a thing or two. Everyone says it'll take a miracle, but that's when Midget starts to realize that even miracles are possible. It's just that sometimes they hurt people who get in the way . . .

'a masterly handling of suspense and cold trickling horror'

Sunday Telegraph